The Uttermost Farthing

A Savant's Vendetta

R. Austin Freeman

The Uttermost Farthing: A Savant's Vendetta

The present edition is a reproduction of previous publication of this classic work. Minor typographical errors may have been corrected without note; however, for an authentic reading experience the spelling, punctuation, and capitalization have been retained from the original text.

ISBN: 978-1-63637-108-5

CONTENTS

CONTENTS

I

THE MOTIVE FORCE

It is not without some misgivings that I at length make public the strange history communicated to me by my lamented friend Humphrey Challoner. The outlook of the narrator is so evidently abnormal, his ethical standards are so remote from those ordinarily current, that the chronicle of his life and actions may not only fail to secure the sympathy of the reader but may even excite a certain amount of moral repulsion. But by those who knew him, his generosity to the poor, and especially to those who struggled against undeserved misfortune, will be an ample set-off to his severity and even ferocity towards the enemies of society.

Humphrey Challoner was a great savant spoiled by untimely wealth. When I knew him he had lapsed into a mere dilettante; at least, so I thought at the time, though subsequent revelations showed him in a rather different light. He had some reputation as a criminal anthropologist and had formerly been well known as a comparative anatomist, but when I made his acquaintance he seemed to be occupied chiefly in making endless additions to the specimens in his private museum. This collection I could never quite understand. It consisted chiefly of human and other mammalian skeletons, all of which presented certain small deviations from the normal; but its object I could never make out—until after his death; and then, indeed, the revelation was a truly astounding one.

I first made Challoner's acquaintance in my professional capacity. He consulted me about some trifling ailment and we took rather a liking to each other. He was a learned man and his learning overlapped my own specialty, so that we had a good deal in common. And his personality interested me deeply. He gave me the impression of a man naturally buoyant, genial, witty, whose life had been blighted by some great sorrow. Ordinarily sad and grave in manner, he exhibited flashes of a grim, fantastic humor that came

1

as a delightful surprise and showed what he had been, and might still have been, but for that tragedy at which he sometimes hinted. Gentle, sympathetic, generous, his universal kindliness had yet one curious exception: his attitude towards habitual offenders against the law was one of almost ferocious vindictiveness.

At the time that I went away for my autumn holiday his health was not quite satisfactory. He made no complaint, indeed he expressed himself as feeling perfectly well; but a certain, indefinable change in his appearance had made me a little uneasy. I said nothing to him on the subject, merely asking him to keep me informed as to his condition during my absence, but it was not without anxiety that I took leave of him.

The habits of London society enable a consultant to take a fairly liberal holiday. I was absent about six weeks, and when I returned and called on Challoner, his appearance shocked me. There was no doubt now as to the gravity of his condition. His head appeared almost to have doubled in size. His face was bloated, his features were thickened, his eyelids puffy and his eyes protruding. He stood, breathing hard from the exertion of crossing the room and held out an obviously swollen hand.

"Well, Wharton," said he, with a strange, shapeless smile, "how do you find me? Don't you think I'm getting a fine fellow? Growing like a pumpkin, by Jove! I've changed the size of my collars three times in a month and the new ones are too tight already." He laughed—as he had spoken—in a thick, muffled voice and I made shift to produce some sort of smile in response to his hideous facial contortion.

"You don't seem to like the novelty, my child," he continued gaily and with another horrible grin. "Don't like this softening of the classic outlines, hey? Well, I'll admit it isn't pretty, but, bless us! what does that matter at my time of life?"

I looked at him in consternation as he stood, breathing quickly, with that uncanny smile on his enormous face. It was highly unprofessional of me, no doubt, but there was little use in attempting to conceal my opinion of his case. Something inside his chest was pressing on the great veins of the neck and arms. That something was either an aneurysm or a solid tumor. A brief

2

examination, to which he submitted with cheerful unconcern, showed that it was a solid growth, and I told him so. He knew some pathology and was, of course, an excellent anatomist, so there was no avoiding a detailed explanation.

"Now, for my part," said he, buttoning up his waistcoat, "I'd sooner have had an aneurysm. There's a finality about an aneurysm. It gives you fair notice so that you may settle your affairs, and then, pop! bang! and the affair's over. How long will this thing take?"

I began to hum and haw nervously, but he interrupted: "It doesn't matter to me, you know, I'm only asking from curiosity; and I don't expect you to give a date. But is it a matter of days or weeks? I can see it isn't one of months."

"I should think, Challoner," I said huskily, "it may be four or five weeks—at the outside."

"Ha!" he said brightly, "that will suit me nicely. I've finished my job and rounded up my affairs generally, so that I am ready whenever it happens. But light your pipe and come and have a look at the museum."

Now, as I knew (or believed I knew) by heart every specimen in the collection, this suggestion struck me as exceedingly odd; but reflecting that his brain might well have suffered some disturbance from the general engorgement, I followed him without remark. Slowly we passed down the corridor that led to the "museum wing," walked through the ill-smelling laboratories (for Challoner prepared the bones of the lower animals himself, though, for obvious reasons, he acquired the human skeletons from dealers) and entered the long room where the main collection was kept.

Here we halted, and while Challoner recovered his breath, I looked round on the familiar scene. The inevitable whale's skeleton—a small sperm whale—hung from the ceiling, on massive iron supports. The side of the room nearest the door was occupied by a long glass case filled with skeletons of animals, all diseased, deformed or abnormal. On the floor-space under the whale stood the skeletons of a camel and an aurochs. The camel was affected with rickets and the aurochs had multiple exostoses or bony tumors. At one end of the room was a large case of skulls, all

3

deformed or asymmetrical; at the other stood a long table and a chest of shallow drawers; while the remaining long side of the room was filled from end to end by a glass case about eight feet high containing a number of human skeletons, each neatly articulated and standing on its own pedestal.

Now, this long case had always been somewhat of a mystery to me. Its contents differed from the other specimens in two respects. First, whereas all the other skeletons and the skulls bore full descriptive labels, these human skeletons were distinguished merely by a number and a date on the pedestal; and, second, whereas all the other specimens illustrated some disease or deformity, these were, apparently, quite normal or showed only some trifling abnormality. They were beautifully prepared and bleached to ivory whiteness, but otherwise they were of no interest, and I could never understand Challoner's object in accumulating such a number of duplicate specimens.

"You think you know this collection inside out," said Challoner, as if reading my thoughts.

"I know it pretty well, I think," was my reply.

"You don't know it at all," he rejoined.

"Oh, come!" I said. "I could write a catalogue of it from memory."

Challoner laughed. "My dear fellow," said he, "you have never seen the real gems of the collection. I am going to show them to you now."

He passed his arm through mine and we walked slowly up the long room; and as we went, he glanced in at the skeletons in the great case with a faint and very horrible smile on his bloated face. At the extreme end I stopped him and pointed to the last skeleton in the case.

"I want you to explain to me, Challoner, why you have distinguished this one by a different pedestal from the others."

As I spoke, I ran my eye along the row of gaunt shapes that filled the great case. Each skeleton stood on a pedestal of ebonized wood on which was a number and a date painted in white, excepting the end one, the pedestal of which was coated with scarlet enamel and the number and date on it in gold lettering.

4

"That specimen," said Challoner, thoughtfully, "is the last of the flock. It made the collection complete. So I marked it with a distinctive pedestal. You will understand all about it when you take over. Now come and look at my gems."

He walked behind the chest of drawers and stood facing the wall which was covered with mahogany paneling. Each panel was about four feet wide by five high, was bordered by a row of carved rosettes and was separated from the adjoining panels by pilasters.

"Now, watch me, Wharton," said he. "You see these two rosettes near the bottom of the panel. You press your thumbs on them, so; and you give a half turn. That turns a catch. Then you do this." He grasped the pilaster on each side of the panel, gave a gentle pull, and panel and pilasters came away bodily, exposing a moderate-sized cupboard. I hastily relieved him of the panel, and, when he had recovered his breath, he began to expound the contents of this curious hiding-place.

"That row of books you will take possession of and examine when my lease falls in. You are my executor and this collection will be yours to keep or give away or destroy, as you think fit. The books consist of a finger-print album, a portrait album, a catalogue and a history of the collection. You will find them all quite interesting. Now I will show you the gems if you will lift those boxes down on to the table."

I did as he asked; lifting down the pile of shallow boxes and placing them, at his direction, side by side on the table. When they were arranged to his satisfaction, he took off the lids with somewhat of a flourish, and I uttered an exclamation of amazement.

The boxes were filled with dolls' heads; at least, such I took them to be. But such dolls! I had never seen anything like them before. So horribly realistic and yet so unnatural! I can only describe the impression they produced by that much-misused word "weird." They were uncanny in the extreme, suggesting to the beholder the severed heads of a company of fantastic, grotesque-looking dwarfs. Let me try to describe them in detail.

Each head was about the size of a small monkey's, that is, about four inches long. It appeared to be made of some fine leather or vellum, remarkably like human skin in texture. The hair in all of them was disproportionately long and very thick, so that it looked somewhat like a paint-brush. But it was undoubtedly human hair. The eyebrows too were unnaturally thick and long and so were the mustache and beard, when present; being composed, as I could plainly see, of genuine mustache and beard hairs of full length and very closely set. Some were made to represent clean-shaven men, and some even showed two or three days' growth of stubble; which stubble was disproportionately long and most unnaturally dense. The eyes of all were closed and the eyelashes formed a thick, projecting brush. But despite the abnormal treatment of the hairy parts, these little heads had the most astonishingly realistic appearance and were, as I have said, excessively weird and rather dreadful in aspect. And, in spite of the closed eyes and set features, each had an expression and character of its own; each, in fact, seemed to be a faithful and spirited portrait of a definite individual. They were upwards of twenty in number, all male and all represented persons of the European type. Each reposed in a little velvet-lined compartment and each was distinguished by a label bearing a number and a date.

I looked up at Challoner and found him regarding me with an inscrutable and hideous smile.

"These are very extraordinary productions, Challoner," said I. "What are they? And what are they made of?"

"Made of, my dear fellow?" said he. "Why, the same as you and I are made of, to be sure."

"Do you mean to say," I exclaimed, "that these little heads are made of human skin?"

"Undoubtedly. Human skin and human hair. What else did you think?"

I looked at him with a puzzled frown and finally said that I did not understand what he meant.

"Have you never heard of the Mundurucú Indians?" he asked.

I shook my head. "What about them?" I asked.

"You will find an account of them in Bates' "Naturalist on the Amazon," and there is a reference to them in Gould and Pyle's "Anomalies.""

6

There was a pause, during which I gazed, not without awe, at the open boxes. Finally I looked at Challoner and asked, "Well?"

"Well, these are examples of the Mundurucú work."

I looked again at the boxes and I must confess that, as my eye traveled along the rows of impassive faces and noted the perfect though diminutive features, the tiny ears, the bristling hair, the frowning eye-brows—so discordant with the placid expression and peacefully closed eyes—a chill of horror crept over me. The whole thing was so unreal, so unnatural, so suggestive of some diabolical wizardry. I looked up sharply at my host.

"Where did you get these things, Challoner?" I asked.

His bloated face exhibited again that strange, inscrutable smile.

"You will find a full account of them in the archives of the museum. Every specimen is fully described there and the history of its acquirement and origin given in detail. They are interesting little objects, aren't they?"

"Very," I replied abstractedly; for I was speculating at the moment on the disagreement between the appearance of the heads and their implied origin. Finally I pointed out the discrepancy.

"But these heads were never prepared by those Indians you speak of."

"Why not?"

"Because they are all Europeans; in fact, most of them look like Englishmen."

"Well? And what about it?" Challoner seemed quietly amused at my perplexity, but at this moment my eye noted a further detail which—I cannot exactly say why—seemed to send a fresh shiver down my spine.

"Look here, Challoner," I said. "Why is this head distinguished from the others? They are all in compartments lined with black velvet and have black labels with white numbers and dates; this one has a compartment lined with red velvet and a red label with a gold number and date, just as in the case of that end skeleton." I glanced across at the case and then it came to me in a flash that the numbers and the dates were identical on both.

Challoner saw that I had observed this and replied: "It is

7

perfectly simple, my dear fellow. That skeleton and this head were acquired on the same day, and with their acquirement my collection was complete. They were the final specimens and I have added nothing since I got them. But in the case of the head there was a further reason for a distinctive setting: it is the gem of the whole collection. Just look at the hair. Take my lens and examine it."

He handed me his lens and I picked the head out of its scarlet nest—it was as light as a cork—and brought it close to my eye. And then, even without the lens, I could see what Challoner meant. The hair presented an excessively rare abnormality; it was what is known as "ringed hair;" that is to say, each hair was marked by alternate light and dark rings.

"You say this is really human hair?" I asked.

"Undoubtedly. And a very fine example of ringed hair; the only one, I may say, that I have ever seen."

"I have never seen a specimen before," said I, laying the little head down in its compartment, "nor," I added, "have I ever seen or heard of anything like these uncanny objects. Won't you tell me where you got them?"

"Not now," said Challoner. "You will learn all about them from the 'Archives,' and very interesting you will find them. And now we'll put them away." He placed the lids on the boxes, and, when I had stowed them away in the cupboard, he made me replace the panel and take a special note of the position of the fastenings for future use.

"Can you stay and have some dinner with me?" he asked, adding, "I am quite presentable at table, still, though I don't swallow very comfortably."

"Yes," I answered, "I will stay with pleasure; I am not officially back at work yet. Hanley is still in charge of my practice."

Accordingly we dined together, though, as far as he was concerned, the dinner was rather an empty ceremony. But he was quite cheerful; in fact, he seemed in quite high spirits, and in the intervals of struggling with his food contrived to talk a little in his quaint, rather grotesquely humorous fashion.

While the meal was in progress, however, our conversation was merely desultory and not very profuse; but when the cloth was

8

removed and the wine set on the table he showed a disposition for more connected talk.

"I suppose I can have a cigar, Wharton? Won't shorten my life seriously, h'm?"

If it would have killed him on the spot, I should have raised no objection. I replied by pushing the box towards him, and, when he had selected a cigar and cut off its end with a meditative air, he looked up at me and said:

"I am inclined to be reminiscent tonight, Wharton; to treat you to a little autobiography, h'm?"

"By all means. You will satisfy your own inclinations and my curiosity at the same time."

"You're a deuced polite fellow, Wharton. But I'm not going to bore you. You'll be really interested in what I'm going to tell you; and especially will you be interested when you come to go through the museum by the light of the little history that you are going to hear. For you must know that my life for the last twenty years has been bound up with my collection. The one is, as it were, a commentary on and an illustration of the other. Did you know that I had ever been married?"

"No," I answered in some surprise; for Challoner had always seemed to me the very type of the solitary, self-contained bachelor.

"I have never mentioned it," said he. "The subject would have been a painful one. It is not now. The malice of sorrow and misfortune loses its power as I near the end of my pilgrimage. Soon I shall step across the border and be out of its jurisdiction forever."

He paused, lit his cigar, took a few labored draughts of the fragrant smoke, and resumed: "I did not marry until I was turned forty. I had no desire to. I was a solitary man, full of my scientific interests and not at all susceptible to the influence of women. But at last I met my late wife and found her different from all other women whom I had seen. She was a beautiful girl, some twenty years younger than I, highly intelligent, cultivated and possessed of considerable property. Of course I was no match for her. I was nothing to look at, was double her age, was only moderately well off and had no special standing either socially or in the world of science. But she married me and, as I may say, she married me

9

handsomely; by which I mean that she always treated our marriage as a great stroke of good fortune for her, as if the advantages were all on her side instead of on mine. As a result, we were absolutely devoted to each other. Our life was all that married life could be and that it so seldom is. We were inseparable. In our work, in our play, in every interest and occupation, we were in perfect harmony. We grudged the briefest moment of separation and avoided all society because we were so perfectly happy with each other. She was a wife in a million; and it was only after I had married her that I realized what a delightful thing it was to be alive. My former existence, looked back on from that time, seemed but a blank expanse through which I had stagnated as a chrysalis lingers on, half alive, through the dreary months of winter.

"We lived thus in unbroken concord, with mutual love that grew from day to day, until two years of perfect happiness had passed.

"And then the end came."

Here Challoner paused, and a look of unutterable sadness settled on his poor, misshapen face. I watched him with an uncomfortable premonition of something disagreeable in the sequel of his narrative as, with his trembling, puffy hand, he re-lighted the cigar that had gone out in the interval.

"The end came," he repeated presently. "The perfect happiness of two human beings was shattered in a moment. Let me describe the circumstances.

"I am usually a light sleeper, like most men of an active mind, but on this occasion I must have slept more heavily than usual. I awoke, however, with somewhat of a start and the feeling that something had happened. I immediately missed my wife and sat up in bed to listen. Faint creakings and sounds of movement were audible from below and I was about to get up and investigate when a door slammed, a bell rang loudly and then the report of a pistol or gun echoed through the house.

"I sprang out of bed and rushed down the stairs. As I reached the hall, someone ran past me in the darkness. There was a blinding flash close to my face and a deafening explosion; and when I recovered my sight, the form of a man appeared for an instant

10

dimly silhouetted in the opening of the street door. The door closed with a bang, leaving the house wrapped in silence and gloom.

"My first impulse was to pursue the man, but it immediately gave way to alarm for my wife. I groped my way into the dining-room and was creeping towards the place where the matches were kept when my bare foot touched something soft and bulky. I stooped to examine it and my outspread hand came in contact with a face.

"I sprang up with a gasp of terror and searched frantically for the matches. In a few moments I had found them and tremblingly struck a light; and the first glimmer of the flame turned my deadly fear into yet more deadly realization. My wife lay on the hearth-rug, her upturned face as white as marble, her half-open eyes already glazing. A great, brown scorch marked the breast of her night-dress and at its center was a small stain of blood.

"She was stone dead. I saw that at a glance. The bullet must have passed right through her heart and she must have died in an instant. That, too, I saw. And though I called her by her name and whispered words of tenderness into her ears; though I felt her pulseless wrists and chafed her hands—so waxen now and chill—I knew that she was gone.

"I was still kneeling beside her, crazed, demented by grief and horror; still stroking her poor white hand, telling her that she was my dear one, my little Kate, and begging her, foolishly, to come back to me, to be my little friend and playmate as of old; still, I say, babbling in the insanity of grief, when I heard a soft step descending the stairs. It came nearer. The door opened and someone stole into the room on tip-toe. It was the housemaid, Harratt. She stood stock still when she saw us and stared and uttered strange whimpering cries like a frightened dog. And then, suddenly, she turned and stole away silently as she had come, and I heard her running softly upstairs. Presently she came down again, but this time she passed the dining-room and went out of the street door. I vaguely supposed she had gone for assistance, but the matter did not concern me. My wife was dead. Nothing mattered now.

"Harratt did not return, however, and I soon forgot her. The death of my dear one grew more real. I began to appreciate it as an actual fact. And with this realization, the question of my own death arose. I took it for granted from the first. The burden of solitary existence was not to be entertained for a moment. The only question was how, and I debated this in leisurely fashion, sitting on the floor with Kate's hand in mine. I had a pistol upstairs and, of course, there were keen-edged scalpels in the laboratory. But, strange as it may appear, the bias of an anatomical training even then opposed the idea of gross mechanical injuries. However, there were plenty of poisons available, and to this method I inclined as more decent and dignified.

"Having settled on the method, I was disposed to put it into practice at once; but then another consideration arose. My wife would have to be buried. By some hands she must be laid in her last resting-place, and those hands could be none other than my own. So I must stay behind for a little while.

"The hours passed on unreckoned until pencils of cold blue daylight began to stream in through the chinks of the shutters and contend with the warm gaslight within. Then another footstep was heard on the stairs and the cook, Wilson, came into the room. She, like the housemaid, stopped dead when she saw my wife's corpse, and stood for an instant staring wildly with her mouth wide open. But only for an instant. The next she was flying out of the front door, rousing the street with her screams.

"The advent of the cook roused me. I knew that the police would arrive soon and I instinctively looked about me to see how this unspeakable thing had happened. I had already noticed that one of my wife's hands—the one that I had not been holding—was clenched, and I now observed that it grasped a little tuft of hair. I drew out a portion of the tuft and looked at it. It was coarse hair, about three inches long and a dull gray in color. I laid it on the clean note-paper in the drawer of the bureau bookcase to examine later, and then glanced around the room. The origin of the tragedy was obvious. The household plate had been taken out of the plate chest in the pantry and laid out on the end of the dining table. There the things stood, their polished surfaces sullied by the greasy finger-marks of the wretch who had murdered my wife. At those

12

tell-tale marks I looked with new and growing interest. Finger-prints, in those days, had not yet been recognized by the public or the police as effective means of identification. But they were well known to scientific men and I had given the subject some attention myself. And the sight of those signs-manual of iniquity had an immediate effect on me; they converted the unknown perpetrator of this horror from a mere abstraction of disaster into a real, living person. With a sudden flush of hate and loathing, I realized that this wretch was even now walking the streets or lurking in his accursed den; and I realized, too, that these marks were, perhaps, the only links that connected him with the foul deed that he had done.

"I looked over the plate quickly and selected a salver and a large, globular teapot, on both of which the prints were very distinct. These I placed in a drawer of the bureau, and, turning the key, dropped it into the pocket of my pajamas. And at that moment the bell rang violently.

"I went to the door and admitted a police constable and the cook. The latter looked at me with evident fear and horror and the constable said, somewhat sternly:

"'This young woman tells me there's something wrong here, sir.'

"I led him into the dining-room—the cook remained at the door, peering in with an ashen face—and showed him my wife's corpse. He took off his helmet and asked rather gruffly how it happened. I gave him a brief account of the catastrophe, on which he made no comment except to remark that the inspector would be here presently.

"The inspector actually arrived within a couple of minutes, accompanied by a sergeant, and the two officers questioned me closely. I repeated my statement and saw at once that they did not believe me; that they suspected me of having committed the murder myself. I noted the fact with dull surprise but without annoyance. It didn't seem to matter to me what they thought.

"They called the cook in and questioned her, but, of course, she knew nothing. Then they sent her to find the housemaid. But the housemaid had disappeared and her outdoor clothes and a

13

large hand-bag had disappeared too; which put a new complexion on the matter. Then the officers examined the plate and looked at the finger-marks on it. The constable discovered the tuft of hair in my poor wife's hand, and the inspector having noted its color and looked rather hard at my hair, put it for safety in a blue envelope, which he pocketed; and I suspect it never saw the light again.

"About this time the police surgeon arrived, but there was nothing for him to do but note the state of the body as bearing on the time at which death took place. The police took possession of some of the plate with a dim idea of comparing the finger-prints with the fingers of the murderer if they should catch him.

"But they never did catch him. Not a vestige of a clue to his identity was ever forthcoming. The housemaid was searched for but never found. The coroner's jury returned a verdict of 'wilful murder' against some person unknown. And that was the end of the matter. I accompanied my dearest to the place where she was laid to rest, where soon I shall join her. And I came back alone to the empty house.

"It is unnecessary for me to say that I did not kill myself. In the interval I had seen things in a new light. It was evident to me from the first that the police would never capture that villain. And yet he had to be captured. He had incurred a debt, and that debt had to be paid. Therefore I remained behind to collect it.

"That was twenty years ago, Wharton; twenty long, gray, solitary years. Many a time have I longed to go to her, but the debt remained unpaid. I have tried to make the time pass by getting my little collection together and studying the very instructive specimens in it; and it has lightened the burden. But all the time I have been working to collect that debt and earn my release."

He paused awhile, and I ventured to ask: "And is the debt paid?"

"At last it is paid."

"The man was caught, then, in the end?"

"Yes. He was caught."

"And I hope," I exclaimed fervently, "that the scoundrel met with his deserts; I mean, that he was duly executed."

"Yes," Challoner answered quietly, "he was executed."

"How did the police discover him, after all?" I asked.

"You will find," said Challoner, "a full account of the affair in the last volume of the 'Museum Archives';" then, noting the astonishment on my face at this amazing statement, he added: "You see, Wharton, the 'Museum Archives' are, in a sense, a personal diary; my life has been wrapped up in the museum and I have associated all the actions of my life with the collection. I think you will understand when you read it. And now let us dismiss these recollections of a ruined life. I have told you my story; I wanted you to hear it from my own lips, and you have heard it. Now let us take a glass of wine and talk of something else."

I looked at my watch and, finding it much later than I had supposed, rose to take my leave.

"I oughtn't to have kept you up like this," I said. "You ought to have been in bed an hour ago."

Challoner laughed his queer muffled laugh. "Bed!" exclaimed he. "I don't go to bed nowadays. Haven't been able to lie down for the last fortnight."

Of course he hadn't. I might have known that. "Well," I said, "at any rate, let me make you comfortable for the night before I go. How do you generally manage?"

"I rig up a head-rest on the edge of the table, pull up the armchair, wrap myself in a rug and sleep leaning forward. I'll show you. Just get down Owen's 'Comparative Anatomy' and stack the volumes close to the edge of the table. Then set up Parker's 'Monograph on the Shoulder-girdle' in a slanting position against them. Fine book, that of Parker's. I enjoyed it immensely when it first came out and it makes a splendid head-rest. I'll go and get into my pajamas while you are arranging the things."

He went off to his adjacent bedroom and I piled up the ponderous volumes on the table and drew up the armchair. When he returned, I wrapped him in a couple of thick rugs and settled him in his chair. He laid his arms on the massive monograph, rested his forehead on them and murmured cheerfully that he should now be quite comfortable until the morning. I wished him "good-night" and walked slowly to the door, and as I held it open I stopped to look back at him. He raised his head and gave me a

15

farewell smile; a queer, ugly smile, but full of courage and a noble patience. And so I left him.

Thereafter I called to see him every day and settled him to rest every night. His disease made more rapid progress even than I had expected; but he was always bright and cheerful, never made any complaint and never again referred to his troubled past.

One afternoon I called a little later than usual, and when the housemaid opened the door I asked her how he was.

"He isn't any better, sir," she answered. "He's getting most awful fat, sir; about the head I mean."

"Where is he now?" I asked.

"He's in the dining-room, sir; I think he's gone to sleep."

I entered the room quietly and found him resting by the table. He was wrapped up in his rugs and his head rested on his beloved monograph. I walked up to him and spoke his name softly, but he did not rouse. I leaned over him and listened, but no sound or movement of breathing was perceptible. The housemaid was right. He had gone to sleep; or, in his own phrase, he had passed out of the domain of sorrow.

II

"NUMBER ONE"

It was more than a week after the funeral of my poor friend Humphrey Challoner that I paid my first regular visit of inspection to his house. I had been the only intimate friend of this lonely, self-contained man and he had made me not only his sole executor but his principal legatee. With the exception of a sum of money to endow an Institute of Criminal Anthropology, he had made me the heir to his entire estate, including his museum. The latter bequest was unencumbered by any conditions. I could keep the collection intact, I could sell it as it stood or I could break it up and distribute the specimens as I chose; but I knew that Challoner's unexpressed wish was that it should be kept together, ultimately to form the nucleus of a collection attached to the Institute.

It was a gray autumn afternoon when I let myself in. A caretaker was in charge of the house, which was otherwise unoccupied, and the museum, which was in a separate wing, seemed strangely silent and remote. As the Yale latch of the massive door clicked behind me, I seemed to be, and in fact was, cut off from all the world. A mysterious, sepulchral stillness pervaded the place, and when I entered the long room I found myself unconsciously treading lightly so as not to disturb the silence; even as one might on entering some Egyptian tomb-chamber hidden in the heart of a pyramid.

I halted in the center of the long room and looked about me, and I don't mind confessing that I felt distinctly creepy. It was not the skeleton of the whale that hung overhead, with its ample but ungenial smile; it was not the bandy-legged skeleton of the rachitic camel, nor that of the aurochs, nor those of the apes and jackals and porcupines in the smaller glass case; nor the skulls that grinned from the case at the end of the room. It was the long row of human skeletons, each erect and watchful on its little pedestal, that occupied the great wall-case: a silent, motionless company of

17

fleshless sentinels, standing in easy postures with unchanging, mirthless grins and seeming to wait for something. That was what disturbed me.

I am not an impressionable man; and, as a medical practitioner, it is needless to say that mere bones have no terrors for me. The skeleton from which I worked as a student was kept in my bedroom, and I minded it no more than I minded the plates in "Gray's Anatomy." I could have slept comfortably in the Hunterian Museum—other circumstances being favorable; and even the gigantic skeleton of Corporal O'Brian—which graces that collection—with that of his companion, the quaint little dwarf, thrown in, would not have disturbed my rest in the smallest degree. But this was different. I had the feeling, as I had had before, that there was something queer about this museum of Challoner's.

I walked slowly along the great wall-case, looking in at the specimens; and in the dull light, each seemed to look out at me as I passed with a questioning expression in his shadowy eye-sockets, as if he would ask, "Do you know who I was?" It made me quite uncomfortable.

There were twenty-five of them in all. Each stood on a small black pedestal on which was painted in white a number and a date; excepting one at the end, which had a scarlet pedestal and gold lettering. Number 1 bore the date 20th September, 1889, and Number 25 (the one with the red pedestal) was dated 13th May, 1909. I looked at this last one curiously; a massive figure with traces of great muscularity, a broad, Mongoloid head with large cheekbones and square eye-sockets. A formidable fellow he must have been; and even now, the broad, square face grinned out savagely from the case.

I turned away with something of a shudder. I had not come here to get "the creeps." I had come for Challoner's journal, or the "Museum Archives" as he called it. The volumes were in the secret cupboard at the end of the room and I had to take out the movable panel to get at them. This presented no difficulty. I found the rosettes that moved the catches and had the panel out in a twinkling. The cupboard was five feet high by four broad and had a well in the bottom covered by a lid, which I lifted and, to my

18

amazement, found the cavity filled with revolvers, automatic pistols, life-preservers, knuckle-dusters and other weapons, each having a little label—bearing a number and a date—tied neatly on it. I shut the lid down rather hastily; there was something rather sinister in that collection of lethal appliances.

The volumes, seven in number, were on the top shelf, uniformly bound in Russia leather and labeled, respectively, "Photographs," "Finger-prints," "Catalogue," and four volumes of "Museum Archives." I was about to reach down the catalogue when my eye fell on the pile of shallow boxes on the next shelf. I knew what they contained and recalled uncomfortably the strange impression that their contents had made on me; and yet a sort of fascination led me to take down the top one—labelled "Series B 5"— and raise the lid. But if those dreadful dolls' heads had struck me as uncanny when poor Challoner showed them to me, they now seemed positively appalling. Small as they were—and they were not as large as a woman's fist—they looked so life-like—or rather, so death-like—that they suggested nothing so much as actual human heads seen through the wrong end of a telescope. There were five in this box, each in a separate compartment lined with black velvet and distinguished by a black label with white lettering; excepting the central one, which rested on scarlet velvet and had a red label inscribed in gold "13th May, 1909."

I gazed at this tiny head in its scarlet setting with shuddering fascination. It had a hideous little face; a broad, brutal face of the Tartar type; and the mop of gray-brown hair, so unhuman in color, and the bristling mustache that stood up like a cat's whiskers, gave it an aspect half animal, half devilish. I clapped the lid on the box, thrust it back on the shelf, and, plucking down the first volume of the "Archives," hurried out of the museum.

That night, when I had rounded up the day's work with a good dinner, I retired to my study, and, drawing an armchair up to the fire, opened the volume. It was a strange document. At first I was unable to perceive the relevancy of the matter to the title, for it seemed to be a journal of Challoner's private life; but later I began to see the connection, to realize, as Challoner had said, that the

19

collection was nothing more than a visible commentary on and illustration of his daily activities.

The volume opened with an account of the murder of his wife and the circumstances leading up to it, written with a dry circumstantiality that was to me infinitely pathetic. It was the forced impassiveness of a strong man whose heart is breaking. There were no comments, no exclamations; merely a formal recital of facts, exhaustive, literal and precise. I need not quote it, as it only repeated the story he had told me, but I will commence my extract at the point where he broke off. The style, as will be seen, is that of a continuous narrative, apparently compiled from a diary; and, as it proceeds, marking the lapse of time, the original dryness of manner gives place to one more animated, more in keeping with the temperament of the writer.

"When I had buried my dear wife, I waited with some impatience to see what the police would do. I had no great expectations. The English police system is more adjusted to offences against property than to those against the person. Nothing had been stolen, so nothing could be traced; and the clues were certainly very slight. It soon became evident to me that the authorities had given the case up. They gave me no hope that the murderer would ever be identified; and, in fact, it was pretty obvious that they had written the case off as hopeless and ceased to interest themselves in it.

"Of course I could not accept this view. My wife had been murdered. The murder was without extenuation. It had been committed lightly to cover a paltry theft. Now, for murder, no restitution is possible. But there is an appropriate forfeit to be paid; and if the authorities failed to exact it, then the duty of its exaction devolved upon me. Moreover, a person who thus lightly commits murder as an incident in his calling is unfit to live in a community of human beings. It was clearly my duty as a good citizen to see that this dangerous person was eliminated.

"This was well enough in theory, but its realization in practice presented considerable difficulties. The police had (presumably) searched for this person and failed to find him. How was I, untrained in methods of detection, to succeed where the experts

20

had been baffled? I considered my resources. They consisted of a silver teapot and a salver which had been handled by the murderer and which, together, yielded a complete set of finger-prints, and the wisp of hair that I had taken from the hand of my murdered wife. It is true that the police also had finger-marked plate and the remainder of the hair and had been unable to achieve anything by their means; but the value of finger-impressions for the purposes of identification is not yet appreciated outside scientific circles.[1] I fetched the teapot and salver from the drawer in which I had secured them and examined them afresh. The teapot had been held in both hands and bore a full set of prints; and these were supplemented by the salver. For greater security I photographed the whole set of the finger-impressions and made platinotype prints which I filed for future reference. Then I turned my attention to the hair. I had already noticed that it was of a dull gray color, but now, when I came to look at it more closely, I found the color so peculiar that I took it to the window and examined it with a lens.

"The result was a most startling discovery. It was ringed hair. The gray appearance was due, not to the usual mingling of white and dark hairs, but to the fact that each separate hair was marked by alternate rings of black and white. Now, variegated hairs are common enough in the lower animals which have a pattern on the fur. The tabby cat furnishes a familiar example. But in man the condition is infinitely rare; whence it was obvious that, with these hairs and the finger-prints, I had the means of infallible identification. But identification involves possession of the person to be identified. There was the difficulty. How was it to be overcome?

"Criminals are vermin. They have the typical characters of vermin; unproductive activity combined with disproportionate destructiveness. Just as a rat will gnaw his way through a Holbein panel, or shred up the Vatican Codex to make a nest, so the professional criminal will melt down priceless medieval plate to sell in lumps for a few shillings. The analogy is perfect.

---

[1] The narrative seems to have been written in 1890. —L.W.

"Now, how do we deal with vermin—with the rat, for instance?

"Do we go down his burrow and reason with him? Do we strive to elevate his moral outlook? Not at all. We induce him to come out. And when he has come out, we see to it that he doesn't go back. In short, we set a trap. And if the rat that we catch is not the one that we wanted, we set it again.

"Precisely. That was the method.

"My housemaid had absconded at the time of the murder; she was evidently an accomplice of the murderer. My cook had left on the same day, having conceived a not unnatural horror of the house. Since then I had made shift with a charwoman. But I should want a housemaid and a cook, and if I acted judiciously in the matter of references, I might get the sort of persons who would help my plans. For there are female rats as well as male.

"But there were certain preliminary measures to be taken. My physical condition had to be attended to. As a young man I was a first-class athlete, and even now I was strong and exceedingly active. But I must get into training and brush up my wrestling and boxing. Then I must fit up some burglar alarms, lay in a few little necessaries and provide myself with a suitable appliance for dealing with the 'catch.'

"This latter I proceeded with at once. To the end of a rod of rhinoceros horn about two feet long I affixed a knob of lead weighing two pounds. I covered the knob with a thickish layer of plaited horsehair, and over this fastened a covering of stout leather; and when I had fitted it with a wrist-strap it looked a really serviceable tool. Its purpose is obvious. It was an improved form of that very crude appliance, the sand-bag, which footpads use to produce concussion of the brain without fracturing the skull. I may describe it as a concussor.

"The preliminary measures were proceeding steadily. I had put in a fortnight's attendance at a gymnasium under the supervision of Professor Schneipp, the Bavarian Hercules; I had practiced the most approved 'knock-outs' known to my instructor, the famous pugilist, Melchizedeck Cohen (popularly known as 'Slimy' Cohen); I had given up an hour a day to studying the management of the concussor with the aid of a punching-ball; the alarms were ready for fixing, and I even had the address of an undoubtedly disreputable housemaid, when a most unexpected thing happened. I got a premature bite. A fellow actually walked into the trap without troubling me to set it.

"It befell thus. I had gone to bed rather early and fallen asleep at once, but about one o'clock I awoke with that unmistakable completeness that heralds a sleepless night. I lit my candle-lamp and looked round for the book that I had been reading in the evening, and then I remembered that I had left it in the museum. Now that book had interested me deeply. It contained the only lucid description that I had met with of the Mundurucú Indians and their curious method of preserving the severed heads of their enemies; a method by which the head—after removal of the bones—was shrunk until it was no larger than a man's fist.

"I got up, and, taking my lamp and keys, made my way to the museum wing of the house, which opened out of the dining-room. I found the book, but, instead of returning immediately, lingered in the museum, looking about the great room and at the unfinished collection and gloomily recalling its associations. The museum was a gift from my wife. She had built it and the big laboratory soon after we were married and many a delightful hour we had spent in it together, arranging the new specimens in the cases. I did not allow her to work in the evil-smelling laboratory, but she had a collection of her own, of land and fresh-water shells (which were cleaner to handle than the bones); and I was pulling out some of the drawers in her cabinet, and, as I looked over the shells, thinking of the happy days when we rambled by the riverside or over furzy commons in search of them, when I became aware of faint sounds of movement from the direction of the dining-room.

"I stepped lightly down the corridor that led to the dining-room and listened. The door of communication was shut, but through it I could distinctly hear someone moving about and could occasionally detect the chink of metal. I ran back to the museum—my felt-soled bedroom slippers made no sound—and, taking the 'concussor' from the drawer in which I had concealed it, thrust it through the waist-band of my pajamas. Then I crept back to the door.

"The sounds had now ceased. I inferred that the burglar—for he could be none other—had gone to the pantry, where the plate-chest was kept. On this I turned the Yale latch and softly opened the door. It is my habit to keep all locks and hinges thoroughly oiled, and consequently the door opened without a sound. There was no one in the dining-room; but one burner of the gas was alight and various articles of silver plate were laid on the table, just as they had been when my wife was murdered. I drew the museum door to—I could not shut it because of the noise the spring latch would have made—and slipped behind a Japanese screen that stood near the dining-room door. I had just taken my place when a stealthy footstep approached along the hall. It entered the room and then there was a faint clink of metal. I peeped cautiously round the screen and looked on the back of a man who was standing by the table on which he was noiselessly depositing a number of spoons and forks and a candlestick. Although his back was towards me, a mirror on the opposite wall gave me a good view of his face; a wooden, expressionless face, such as I have since learned to associate with the English habitual criminal; the penal servitude face, in fact.

"He was a careful operator. He turned over each piece thoroughly, weighing it in his hand and giving especial attention to the hall-mark. And, as I watched him, the thought came into my mind that, perchance, this was the very wretch who had murdered my wife, come back for the spoil that he had then had to abandon. It was quite possible, even likely, and at the thought I felt my cheeks flush and a strange, fierce pleasure, such as I had never felt before, swept into my consciousness. I could have laughed aloud, but I did not. Also, I could have knocked him down with perfect ease as he stood, but I did not. Why did I not? Was it a vague, sporting sense of fairness? Or was it a catlike instinct impelling me to play with my quarry? I cannot say. Only I know that the idea of dealing him a blow from behind did not attract me.

"Presently he shuffled away (in list slippers) to fetch a fresh cargo. Then some ferociously playful impulse led me to steal out of my hiding-place and gather up a number of spoons and forks, a salt-cellar, a candlestick and an entree-dish and retire again behind the screen. Then my friend returned with a fresh consignment; and as he was anxiously looking over the fresh pieces, I crept silently out at the other end of the screen, out of the open doorway and down the hall to the pantry. Here a lighted candle showed the plate-chest open and half empty, with a few pieces of plate on a side table. Quickly but silently I replaced in the chest the spoons and other pieces that I had collected, and then stole back to my place behind the screen and resumed my observations.

"My guest was quite absorbed in his task. He had a habit—common, I believe, among 'old lags'—of talking to himself; and very poor stuff his conversation was, though it was better than his arithmetic, as I gathered from his attempts to compute the weight of the booty. Anon, he retired for another consignment, and once more I came out and gathered up a little selection from his stock; and when he returned laden with spoil, I went off, as before, and put the articles back in the plate-chest.

"These manoeuvres were repeated a quite incredible number of times. The man must have been an abject blockhead, as I believe most professional criminals are. His lack of observation was astounding. It is true that he began to be surprised and rather bewildered. He even noted that 'there seemed a bloomin' lot of 'em;' and the quality of his arithmetical feats and his verbal enrichments became, alike, increasingly lurid. I believe he would have gone on until daylight if I had not tried him too often with a Queen Anne teapot. It was that teapot, with its conspicuous urn design, that finally disillusioned him. I had just returned from putting it back in the chest for the third time when he missed it; and he announced the discovery with a profusion of perfectly unnecessary and highly inappropriate adjectives.

"'Naa, then!' he exclaimed truculently, 'where's that blimy teapot gone to? Hay? I put that there teapot down inside that there hontry-dish—and where's the bloomin' hontry? Bust me if that ain't gone to!'

"He stood by the table scratching his bristly head and looking the picture of ludicrous bewilderment. I watched him and meanwhile debated whether or not I should take the opportunity to knock him down. That was undoubtedly the proper course. But I could not bring myself to do it. A spirit of wild mischief possessed me; a strange, unnatural buoyancy and fierce playfulness that impelled me to play insane, fantastic tricks. It was a singular phenomenon. I seemed suddenly to have made the acquaintance of a hitherto unknown moiety of a dual personality.

"The burglar stood awhile, muttering idiotically, and then shuffled off to the pantry. I followed him out into the dark hall and, taking my stand behind a curtain, awaited his return. He came back presently, and, by the glimmer of light from the open door, I could see that he had the teapot and the 'hontry.' Now some previous tenant had fitted the dining-room door with two external bolts; I cannot imagine why; but the present circumstances suggested a use for them. As soon as the burglar was inside, I crept forward and quietly shut the door, shooting the top bolt.

"That roused my friend. He rushed at the door and shook it like a madman; he cursed with incredible fluency and addressed me in terms which it would be inadequate to describe as rude. Then I silently shot the bottom bolt and noisily drew back the top one. He thought I had unbolted the door, and when he found that I had not, his language became indescribable.

"There was a second door to the dining-room also opening into the hall at the farther end. My captive seemed suddenly to remember this, for he made a rush for it. But so did I; and, the hall being unobstructed by furniture, I got there first and shot the top bolt. He wrenched frantically at the handle and addressed me with strange and unseemly epithets. I repeated the manoeuvre of pretending to unbolt the door, and smiled as I heard him literally dancing with frenzy inside. It seemed highly amusing at the time, though now, viewed retrospectively, it looks merely silly.

"Quite suddenly his efforts ceased and I heard him shuffle away. I returned to the other door, but he made no fresh attempt on it. I listened, and hearing no sound, bethought me of the open door of the museum. Probably he had gone there to look for a way out. This would never do. The plate I cared not a fig for, but the museum specimens were a different matter; and he might damage them from sheer malice.

"I unbolted the door, entered and shut it again, locking it on the inside and dropping the key into my pocket. I had just done so when he appeared at the museum door, eyeing me warily and unobtrusively slipping a knuckle-duster on his left hand. I had noted that he was not left-handed and drew my own conclusions as to what he meant to do with his right. We stood for some seconds facing each other and then he began to edge towards the door. I drew aside to let him pass and he ran to the door and turned the handle. When he found the door locked he was furious. He advanced threateningly with his left hand clenched, but then drew back. Apparently, my smiling exterior, coupled with my previous conduct, daunted him. I think he took me for a lunatic; in fact, he hinted as much in coarse, ill-chosen terms. But his vocabulary was very limited, though quaint.

"We exchanged a few remarks and I could see that he did not like the tone of mine. The fact is that the sight of the knuckle-duster had changed my mood. I no longer felt playful. He had recalled me to my original purpose. He expressed a wish to leave the house and to know 'what my game was.' I replied that he was my game and that I believed that I had bagged him, whereupon he rushed at me and aimed a vicious blow at my head with his armed left fist, which, if it had come home, would have stretched me senseless. But it did not. I guarded it easily and countered him so that he staggered back gasping.

"That made him furious. He came at me like a wild beast, with his mouth open and his armed fist flourished aloft as if he would annihilate me. I tried to deal with him by the methods of Mr. Slimy Cohen, but it was useless. He was no boxer and he had a knuckle-duster. Consequently we grabbed one another like a pair of monkeys and sought to inflict unorthodox injuries. He struggled and writhed and growled and kicked and even tried to bite; while I kept, as far as I could, control of his wrists and waited my opportunity. It was a most undignified affair. We staggered to and fro, clawing at one another; we gyrated round the room in a wild, unseemly waltz; we knocked over the chairs, we bumped against the table, we banged each other's heads against the walls; and all the time, as my adversary growled and showed his teeth like a savage dog, I was sensible of a strange feeling of physical enjoyment such as one might experience in some strenuous game. I seemed to have acquired a new and unfamiliar personality.

"But the knuckle-duster was a complication; for it was his right hand that I had to watch; and yet I could not afford to free for an instant his left, armed as it was with that shabbiest of weapons. Hence I hung on to his wrists while he struggled to wrench them free, and we pulled one another backwards and forwards and round and round in the most absurd and amateurish manner, each trying to trip the other up and failing at every attempt. At last, in the course of our gyrations, we bumped through the open door into the passage leading to the museum; and here we came down together with a crash that shook the house.

"As ill luck would have it, I was underneath; but, in spite of the shock of the fall, I still managed to keep hold of his wrists, though I had some trouble to prevent him from biting my hands and face. So our position was substantially unchanged, and we were still wriggling chaotically when a hasty step was heard descending the stairs. The burglar paused for an instant to listen and then, with a sudden effort, wrenched away his right hand, which flew to his hip-pocket and came out grasping a small revolver. Instantly I struck up with my left and caught him a smart blow under the chin, which dislodged him; and as he rolled over there was a flash and a report, accompanied by the shattering of glass and followed immediately by the slamming of the street door. I let go his left hand, and, rising to my knees, grabbed the revolver with my own left, while, with my right, I whisked out the concussor and aimed a vigorous blow at the top of his head. The padded weight came down without a sound—excepting the click of his teeth—and the effect was instantaneous. I rose, breathing quickly and eminently satisfied with the efficiency of my implement until I noticed that the unconscious man was bleeding slightly from the ear; which told me that I had struck too hard and fractured the base of the skull.

"However, my immediate purpose was to ascertain whether

28

this was or was not the man whom I wanted. In the passage it was too dark to see either his finger-tips or the minute texture of his hair; but my candle-lamp, with its parabolic reflector, would give ample light. I ran through into the museum, where it was still burning, and, catching it up, ran back with it; but I had barely reached the prostrate figure when I heard someone noisily opening the street door with a latch-key. The charwoman had returned, no doubt, with the police.

"I am rather obscure as to what I meant to do. I think I had no definitely-formed intentions but acted more or less automatically, impelled by the desire to identify the burglar. What I did was to close the museum door very quietly, with the aid of the key, unlock the dining-room door and open it.

"A police sergeant, a constable and a plain-clothes officer entered and the charwoman lurked in the dark background.

"'Have they got away?' the sergeant demanded.

"'There was only one,' I said.

"At this the officers bustled away and I heard them descending to the basement. The charwoman came in and looked gloatingly at my battered countenance, which bore memorials of every projecting corner of the room.

"'It's a pity you come down, sir,' said she. 'You might have been murdered same as what your poor lady was. It's better to let them sort of people alone. That's what I say. Let 'em alone and they'll go home, as the sayin' is.'

"There was considerable truth in these observations, especially the last. I acknowledged it vaguely, while the woman cast fascinated glances round the disordered room. Then two of the officers returned and took up the enquiry to an accompaniment of distant police whistles from the back of the house.

"'I needn't ask if you saw the man,' said the plain-clothes officer, with a faint grin.

"'No, you're right,' said the sergeant. 'He set upon you properly, sir. Seems to have been a lively party.' He glanced round the room and added: 'Fired a pistol, too, your housekeeper tells me.'

"I nodded at the shattered mirror but made no comment, and the officer, remarking that I 'seemed a bit shaken up,' proceeded with his investigations. I watched the two men listlessly. I was not much interested in them. I was thinking of the man on the other side of the museum door and wondering if he had ringed hair.

"Presently the plain-clothes officer made a discovery. 'Hallo,' said he, 'here's a carpet bag.' He drew it out from under the table and hoisted it up under the gaslight to examine it; and then he burst into a loud and cheerful laugh.

"'What's up?' said the sergeant.

"'Why, it's Jimmy Archer's bag.'

"'No!'

"'Fact. He showed it to me himself. It was given to him by the 'Discharged Prisoners' Aid Society' to carry his tools in. Ha! Ha! O Lord!'

"The sergeant examined the bag with an appreciative grin, which broadened as his colleague lifted out a brace, a pad of bits, a folding jimmy and a few other trifles. I made a mental note of the burglar's name, and then my interest languished again. The two officers looked over the room together, tried the museum door and noted that it had not been tampered with; turned over the plate and admonished me on the folly of leaving it so accessible; and finally departed with the promise to bring a detective-inspector in the morning, and meanwhile to leave a constable to guard the house.

"I would gladly have dispensed with that constable, especially as he settled himself in the dining-room and seemed disposed to converse, which I was not. His presence shut me off from the museum. I could not open the door, for the burglar was lying just inside. It was extremely annoying. I wanted to make sure that the man was really dead, and, especially, I wanted to examine his hair and to compare his finger-prints with the set that I had in the museum. However, it could not be helped. Eventually I took my candle-lamp from the sideboard and went up to bed, leaving the constable seated in the easy-chair with a box of cigars, a decanter of whiskey and a siphon of Apollinaris at his elbow.

"I remained awake a long time cogitating on the situation. Was the man whom I had captured the right man? Had I accomplished my task, and was I now at liberty to 'determine,' as the lawyers say, the lease of my ruined life? That was a question which the morning light would answer; and meanwhile one thing was clear: I had fairly committed myself to the disposal of the dead burglar. I could not produce the body now; I should have to get rid of it as best I could.

"Of course, the problem presented no difficulty. There was a fire-clay furnace in the laboratory in which I had been accustomed to consume the bulky refuse of my preparations. A hundredweight or so of anthracite would turn the body into undistinguishable ash; and yet—well, it seemed a wasteful thing to do. I have always been rather opposed to cremation, to the wanton destruction of valuable anatomical material. And now I was actually proposing, myself, to practice that which I had so strongly deprecated. I reflected. Here was a specimen delivered at my very door, nay, into the very precincts of my laboratory. Why should I destroy it? Could I not turn it to some useful account in the advancement of science?

"I turned this question over at length. Here was a specimen. But a specimen of what? I am no mere curio-monger, no collector of frivolous and unmeaning trifles. A specimen must illustrate some truth. Now what truth did this specimen illustrate? The question, thus stated, brought forth its own answer in a flash.

"Criminal anthropology is practically an unillustrated science. A few paltry photographs, a few mouldering skulls of forgotten delinquents (such as that of Charlotte Corday), form the entire material on which criminal anthropologists base their unsatisfactory generalizations. But here was a really authentic specimen with a traceable life-history. It ought not to be lost to science. And it should not be.

"Presently my thoughts took a new turn. I had been deeply interested in the account that I had read of the ingenious method by which the Mundurucús used to preserve the heads of their slain enemies. The book was unfortunately still in the museum, but I had read the account through, and now recalled it. The Mundurucú warrior, when he had killed an enemy, cut off his head with a broad bamboo knife and proceeded to preserve it thus: First he soaked it for a time in some non-oxidizable vegetable oil; then he extracted the bone and the bulk of the muscles somewhat as a bird-stuffer extracts the body from the skin. He then filled up the cavity with hot pebbles and hung the preparation up to dry.

"By repeating the latter process many times, a gradual and symmetrical shrinkage was produced until the head had dwindled to the size of a man's fist or even smaller, leaving the features, however, practically unaltered. Finally he decorated the little head with bright-colored feathers—the Mundurucús were very clever at feather work—and fastened the lips together with a string, by which the head was suspended from the eaves of his hut or from the beams of the council house.

"It was highly ingenious. The question was whether heads so preserved would be of any use for the study of facial characters. I had intended to get a dead monkey from Jamrach's and experiment in the process. But now it seemed that the monkey would be unnecessary if only the preparation could be produced without injuring the skull; and I had no doubt that, with due care and skill, it could.

"At daybreak I went down to the dining-room. The policeman was dozing in his chair; there was a good deal of cigar-ash about, and the whiskey-decanter was less full than it had been, though not unreasonably so. I roused up the officer and dismissed him with a final cigar and what he called an 'eye-opener'—about two fluid-ounces. When he had gone I let myself into the museum lobby. The burglar was quite dead and beginning to stiffen. That was satisfactory; but was he the right man? I snipped off a little tuft of hair and carried it to the laboratory where the microscope stood on the bench under its bell-glass. I laid one or two hairs on a slide with a drop of glycerine and placed the slide on the stage of the microscope. Now was the critical moment. I applied my eye to the instrument and brought the objective into focus.

"Alas! The hairs were uniformly colored with brown pigment! He was the wrong man.

"It was very disappointing. I really need not have killed him, though under the circumstances there was nothing to regret on that score. He would not have died in vain. Alive he was merely a nuisance and a danger to the community, whereas in the form of museum preparations he might be of considerable public utility.

"Under the main bench in the laboratory was a long cupboard containing a large zinc-lined box or tank in which I had been accustomed to keep the specimens which were in process of preparation. I brought the burglar into the laboratory and deposited him in the tank, shutting the air-tight lid and securing it with a padlock. For further security I locked the cupboard, and, when I had washed the floor of the lobby and dried it with methylated spirit, all traces of the previous night's activities were obliterated. If the police wanted to look over the museum and laboratory, they were now quite at liberty to do so.

"I have mentioned that, during the actual capture of this burglar, I seemed to develop an entirely alien personality. But the change was only temporary, and I had now fully recovered my normal temperament, which is that of a careful, methodical and eminently cautious man. Hence, as I took my breakfast and planned out my procedure, an important fact made itself evident. I should presently have in my museum a human skeleton which I should have acquired in a manner not recognized by social conventions or even by law. Now, if I could place myself in a position to account for that skeleton in a simple and ordinary way, it might, in the future, save inconvenient explanations.

"I decided to take the necessary measures without delay, and accordingly, after a rather tedious interview with the detective-inspector (whom I showed over the entire house, including the museum and laboratory), I took a cab to Great St. Andrew Street, Seven Dials, where resided a well-known dealer in osteology. I did not, of course, inform him that I had come to buy an understudy for a deceased burglar. I merely asked for an articulated skeleton, to stand and not to hang (hanging involves an unsightly suspension ring attached to the skull). I looked over his stock with a steel measuring-tape in my hand, for a skeleton of about the right size—sixty-three inches—but I did not mention that size was a special object. I told him that I wished for one that would illustrate racial characters, at which he smiled—as well he might, knowing that his skeletons were mostly built up of assorted bones of unknown origin.

"I selected a suitable skeleton, paid for it, (five pounds) and took care to have a properly drawn invoice, describing the goods and duly dated and receipted. I did not take my purchase away with me; but it arrived the same day, in a funeral box, which the detective-inspector, who happened to be in the house at the time, kindly assisted me to unpack.

"My next proceeding was to take a set of photographs of the deceased, including three views of the face, a separate photograph of each ear, and two aspects of the hands. I also took a complete set of finger-prints. Then I was ready to commence operations in earnest."

The rest of Challoner's narrative relating to Number One is of a highly technical character and not very well suited to the taste of lay readers. The final result will be understood by the following quotation from the museum catalogue:

"Specimens Illustrating Criminal Anthropology.

"Series A. Osteology.

"1. Skeleton of burglar, aged 37. ♂. Height 63 inches. (James Archer.)

"This specimen was of English parentage, was a professional burglar, a confirmed recidivist, and—since he habitually carried fire-arms—a potential homicide. His general intelligence appears to have been of a low order, his manual skill very imperfect (he was a gas-fitter by trade but never regularly employed). He was nearly illiterate and occasionally but not chronically alcoholic.

"Cranial capacity 1594 cc. Cephalic index 76.8.

"For finger-prints see Album D 1, p. 1. For facial characters see Album E 1, pp. 1, 2 and 3, and Series B (dry, reduced preparations). Number 1."

I closed the two volumes—the Catalogue and the Archives—and meditated on the amazing story that they told in their unemotional, matter-of-fact style. Was poor Challoner mad? Had he an insane obsession on the subject of crime and criminals? Or was he, perchance, abnormally sane, if I may use the expression? That his outlook was not as other men's was obvious. Was it a rational outlook or that of a lunatic?

I cannot answer the question. Perhaps a further study of his Archives may throw some fresh light on it.

III

THE HOUSEMAID'S FOLLOWERS

The contrast in effect between suspicion and certainty is very curious to observe. When I had walked through the private museum of my poor friend Challoner and had looked at the large collection of human skeletons that it contained, a suspicion that there was something queer about those skeletons had made me quite uncomfortable. Now, after reading his first narrative, I knew all about them. They were the relics of criminals whom he had taken red-handed and preserved for the instruction of posterity. Thus were my utmost suspicions verified, and yet, strange as it may seem, with the advent of certainty, my horror of them vanished. Even the hideous little doll-like heads induced but a passing shudder. Vague, half superstitious awe gave place to scientific interest.

I took an early opportunity of renewing my acquaintance with the astonishing and gruesome "Museum Archives." The second narrative was headed "Anthropological Series, 2, 3 and 4." It exhibited the same singular outlook as the first, showing that to Challoner the criminal had not appeared to be a human being at all, but merely a sub-human form, anatomically similar to man.

"The acquisition of Specimen Number One," it began, "gave me considerable occupation, both bodily and mental. As I labored from day to day rendering the osseous framework of the late James Archer fit for exhibition in a museum case, I reflected on the future to which recent events had committed me. I had been, as it were, swept away on the tide of circumstance. The death of this person had occurred by an inadvertence, and accident had thrown on me the onus of disposing of the remains. I had solved that difficulty by converting the deceased into a museum specimen. So far, well, but what of the future?

"My wife had been murdered by a criminal. The remainder of my life—short, I hoped—was to be spent in seeking that criminal.

But the trap that I set to catch him would probably catch other criminals first; and since the available method of identification could not be applied to newly-acquired specimens while in the living state, it followed that each would have to be reduced to the condition in which identification would be possible. And if, on inspection, the specimen acquired proved to be not the one sought, I should have to add it to the collection and rebait the trap. That was evidently the only possible plan.

"But before embarking on it I had to consider its ethical bearings. Of the legal position there was no question. It was quite illegal. But that signified nothing. There are recent human skeletons in the Natural History Museum; every art school in the country has one and so have many board schools. What is the legal position of the owners of those human remains? It will not bear investigation. As to the Hunterian Museum, it is a mere resurrectionist's legacy. That the skeleton of O'Brian was obtained by flagrant body-snatching is a well-known historical fact, but one at which the law, very properly, winks. Obviously the legal position was not worth considering.

"But the ethical position? To me it looked quite satisfactory, though clearly at variance with accepted standards. For the attitude of society towards the criminal appears to be that of a community of stark lunatics. In effect, society addresses the professional criminal somewhat thus:

"'You wish to practice crime as a profession, to gain a livelihood by appropriating—by violence or otherwise—the earnings of honest and industrious men. Very well, you may do so on certain conditions. If you are skilful and cautious you will not be molested. You may occasion danger, annoyance and great loss to honest men with very little danger to yourself unless you are clumsy and incautious; in which case you may be captured. If you are, we shall take possession of your person and detain you for so many months or years. During that time you will inhabit quarters better than you are accustomed to; your sleeping-room will be kept comfortably warm in all weathers; you will be provided with clothing better than you usually wear; you will have a sufficiency of excellent food; expensive officials will be paid to take charge of you;

36

selected medical men will be retained to attend to your health; a chaplain (of your own persuasion) will minister to your spiritual needs and a librarian will supply you with books. And all this will be paid for by the industrious men whom you live by robbing. In short, from the moment that you adopt crime as a profession, we shall pay all your expenses, whether you are in prison or at large.' Such is the attitude of society; and I repeat it is that of a community of madmen.

"How much better and more essentially moral is my plan! I invite the criminal to walk into my parlor. He walks in, a public nuisance and a public danger; and he emerges in the form of a museum preparation of permanent educational value.

"Thus I reflected and mapped out my course of action as I worked at what I may call the foundation specimen of my collection. The latter kept me busy for many days, but I was very pleased with the result when it was finished. The bones were of a good color and texture, the fracture of the skull, when carefully joined with fish-glue, was quite invisible, and, as to the little dried preparation of the head, it was entirely beyond my expectations. Comparing it with the photographs taken after death, I was delighted to find that the facial characters and even the expression were almost perfectly retained.

"It was a red-letter day when I put Number One in the great glass case and took out the skeleton that I had bought from the dealer to occupy its place until it was ready. The substitute was no longer needed and I accordingly dismantled it and destroyed it piecemeal in the furnace, crushing the calcined bones into unrecognizable fragments.

"Meanwhile I had been pushing on my preparations for further captures. A large, mahogany-faced safe was fixed in the dining-room to contain the silver; a burglar alarm was fitted under the floor in front of the safe and connected with a trembler-drum that was kept (with the concussor and a few other appliances) locked in a hanging cupboard at my bed-head, ready to be switched on and placed under my pillow at night. I secretly purchased a quantity of paste jewelry—bracelets, tiaras, pendants and such like glittering trash—and when everything was ready I engaged two new servants of decidedly queer antecedents. I was at first a little doubtful about the cook, but the housemaid was a certainty from the outset. Her character from her late reverend and philanthropic employer, urging me as a Christian man (which I was not) to 'give her another chance,' made that perfectly clear.

"I gave her another chance, though not quite of the kind that the reverend gentleman meant. Two days after her arrival I directed her to clean the plate and handed her the key of the safe, of which I have reason to believe that she took a squeeze with a piece of dough. The sham diamonds were locked in a separate division of the safe, but I introduced them to her by taking them out in her presence, spreading them on the table and ostentatiously cleaning their rolled-gold settings with a soft brush. They certainly made a gorgeous and glittering show. I could not have distinguished them from real diamonds; and as for Susan Slodger—that was the housemaid's name—her eyes fairly bulged with avarice.

"It was less than a week after this that the next incident occurred. I was lying in bed, dozing fitfully but never losing consciousness. I slept badly at that time, for memories which I avoided by day would come crowding on me in the darkness. I would think of my lost happiness, of my poor, murdered wife and of the wretch who had so lightly crushed out her sweet life as one would kill an inconvenient insect; and the thoughts filled me alternately with unutterable sadness that banished sleep or with profound anger that urged me to seek justice and retribution.

"The long-case clock on the stair had just struck two when the trembler-drum beneath my pillow suddenly broke into a prolonged roll. Someone was standing in front of the safe in the dining-room. I rose quietly, switched off the drum, replaced it in the hanging cupboard, and, taking from the same receptacle the concussor and a small leather bag filled with shot and attached to a long coil of fishing-line, softly descended the stairs. On the mid-way landing I laid down the shot-bag and paid out the coil of line as I descended the next flight. In the hall I paused for a few seconds to listen. Both the doors of the dining-room were shut, but I could hear faint sounds within. I approached the door further from the street and carefully grasped the knob. The locks and hinges I knew were thoroughly oiled, for I had attended to them daily in common with all the other doors in the lower part of the house. I turned the knob slowly and made gentle pressure on the door, which presently began to open without a sound. As it opened I became aware of a low muttering, and caught distinctly the half-whispered words, 'Better try the pick first, Fred.'

"So there was more than one at any rate.

"When the door was wide enough open to admit my head, I looked in. One burner of the gas was alight but turned very low, though it gave enough light for me to see three men standing before the safe. Three were rather more than I had bargained for. Number One, by himself, had given me a good deal of occupation, both during and after the capture. Three might prove a little beyond my powers. And yet, if I could only manage them, they would make a handsome addition to my collection. I watched them and turned over the ways and means of dealing with them. Evidently the essence of the strategy required was to separate them and deal with them in detail. But how was it to be done?

"I watched the three men with their heads close together looking into the safe. The door stood wide open and a key in the lock explained the procedure so far. One of the men held an electric bulls-eye lamp, the light of which was focussed on the keyhole of the jewel-compartment, into which another had just introduced a skeleton key.

At this moment, the third man turned his head. By the dim light I could see that he was looking, with a distinctly startled expression, in my direction; in fact, I seemed to meet his eye; but, knowing that I was in complete darkness in the shadow of the door, I remained motionless.

"'Fred,' he whispered hoarsely, 'the door's open.'

"The other two men looked round sharply, and one of them — presumably Fred — retorted gruffly, 'Then go and shut it. And don't make no bloomin' row.'

"The man addressed felt in his pocket and advanced stealthily across the room. His feet were encased in list slippers and his tread was perfectly noiseless. As he approached I backed away, and grasping the newel-post of the staircase gave it a sharp pull, whereat the whole of the balusters creaked loudly. Then I slipped behind the curtain that partly divided the hall, poised the concussor as a golf-player poises his club, and gathered in the slack of the fishing-line.

"The burglar's head appeared dimly in silhouette against the faint light from within. He listened for a moment and then peered out into the dark hall. The opportunity seemed excellent if I could only lure him a little farther out. In any case, he must not be allowed to retire and shut the door.

"I gave a steady pull at the fishing-line. The shot-bag slid over the carpet on the landing above with a sound remarkably like that of a stealthy footstep.

"The burglar looked up sharply and raised his hand; and against the dimly-lighted wall of the dining-room I saw the silhouette of a pointed revolver. The practice of carrying firearms seems to be growing amongst the criminal classes, perhaps by reason of the increasing number of American criminals who visit this country. At any rate, the matter should be dealt with by appropriate legislation.

"The burglar then stood looking out with his revolver pointed up the stairs. I was about to give another tweak at the fishing-line when an unmistakable creak came from the upper stairs. I think this somewhat reassured my friend, for I heard him mutter that 'he supposed it was them dam girls.' He stepped cautiously outside the door, and, fumbling in his pocket, produced a little electric bulls-eye, the light of which he threw up the stairs.

"The opportunity was perfect. Against the circle of light produced by his lamp his head stood out black and distinct, its back towards me, one outstanding ear serving to explain what I may call the constructive details of the flat, dark shape.

"With my left hand I silently held aside the curtain and took a careful aim. Remembering the mishap with Number One, I selected the right parietal eminence, an oblique impact on which would be less likely to injure the base of the skull than a vertical blow. But I put my whole strength into the stroke, and when the padded weight descended on the spot selected, the burglar doubled up as if struck by lightning.

40

"The impact of the concussor was silent enough, but the man fell with a resounding crash, and the revolver and lamp flew from his hands and rattled noisily along the floor of the hall. The instant I had struck the blow I ran lightly up the hall and softly turned the knob of the farther door. Fortunately the two men in the room were too much alarmed to rush out into the hall, or, with the aid of their lamp, they would have seen me. But they were extremely cautious. I thrust my head in at the door and from the dark end of the room I could see them peering out of the other door and listening intently. After a short interval they tip-toed out into the hall and I lost sight of them.

"Close to the farther door was a large, four-fold Japanese screen. It had sheltered me in my last adventure and I thought it might do so again, as the prostrate burglar was lying a couple of yards past the opening of the door and his two friends were probably examining him. Accordingly I stepped softly along the room and took up a position behind the screen in a recess of the folds. My movements had evidently been unobserved and my new position enabled me to peep out into the hall—at some risk of being seen—and to hear all that passed.

"For the moment there was nothing to hear but a faint rustling from the two men and an occasional creak from the upper stairs. But presently I caught a hoarse whisper.

"'Dam funny. He seems to be dead.'

"'Yus; he do look like it,' the other agreed and then added optimistically, 'but p'raps he's only took queer.'

"'Dam!' was the impatient rejoinder. 'I tell yer he's dead— dead as a pork chop.'

"There was another silence and then, in a yet softer whisper, a voice asked:

"'D'yer think somebody's been and done 'im in, Fred?'

"'Don't see no marks,' answered Fred; 'besides there ain't no one here. Hallo! what's that?'

"'That' was a loud creak on the upper stairs near the first-floor landing, doubtless emanating from Miss Slodger or the cook. I have no doubt that these sounds of stealthy movement were highly disturbing to the burglars, especially in the present circumstances.

And so it appeared, for the answer came in an obviously frightened whisper: 'There's someone on the stairs, Fred. Let's hook it. This job ain't no class.'

"'What!' was the indignant reply. "Ook it and leave all that stuff. Not me! Nor you neither. There's more'n what one of us can carry. And you put away that barker or else you'll be lettin' it off and bringin' in the coppers. D'ye 'ear?'

"'Ain't going to be done in the dark same as what Joe's been,' the other whispered sulkily. 'If anyone comes down 'ere, I pots 'im.'

"At this moment there was another very audible creak from above, and then followed rapidly a succession of events which I subsequently disentangled, but which, at the time, were involved in utter confusion. What actually happened was that Fred had begun boldly to ascend the stairs, in some way missing the fishing-line, and being closely followed by his more nervous comrade. The latter, less fortunate, caught his foot in the line, stumbled, tightened the line and brought the shot-bag hopping down the stairs. What I heard was the sound of the stumble, followed by the quick thud, thud, of the descending shot-bag, exactly resembling the footfalls of a heavy man running down the stairs barefoot. Then came two revolver shots in quick succession, a shower of plaster, a hoarse cry, a heavy fall, and, from above, a loud scuffling followed by the slamming of a door and the noisy turning of a key; a brief interval of silence and then a quavering whisper.

"'I ain't 'it yer, Fred, 'ave I?'

"To this question there was no answer but a gurgling groan. I stepped out from my hiding-place, passed through the open doorway and stole softly along the hall, guided by the sound of the survivor extricating himself from his fallen comrade. A few paces from him I halted with the concussor poised ready to strike and listened to his fumbling and scuffling. Suddenly a bright light burst forth. He had found Fred's electric lantern, which was, oddly enough, uninjured by the fall (it had a metal filament, as I subsequently ascertained).

"The circle of light from the bulls-eye, quivering with the tremor of the hand which held the lantern, embraced the figure of the injured burglar, huddled in a heap at the foot of the stairs and still twitching at intervals. It could not have been a pleasant sight to his companion. The greenish-white face with its staring eyes and blood-stained lips stood out in the bright light from its background of black darkness with the vivid intensity of some ghastly wax-work.

"The surviving burglar stood petrified, stooping over his comrade, with the lantern in one shaking hand and the revolver still grasped in the other; and as he stood, he poured out, in a curious, whimpering undertone, an unending torrent of incoherent blasphemies, as appears to be the habit of that type of man when frightened. I stepped silently behind him and looked over his shoulder at the expiring criminal, speculating on what he would do next. At the moment he was paralyzed and imbecile with terror, and I had a strong inclination to dispatch him then and there; but the same odd impulse that I had noticed on the last occasion constrained me to dally with him. Again I was possessed by a strange, savage playfulness like that which impels a cat or leopard to toy daintily and tenderly with its prey for a while before the final scrunch.

"We remained thus motionless for more than half a minute in a silence broken only by his blasphemous mutterings. Then, quite suddenly, he stood up and began to flash his lantern on the stairs and about the hall until at length its light fell full on my face which was within a foot of his own. And at that apparition he uttered a most singular cry, like that of a young goat, and started back. Another moment and he would have raised his pistol arm, but I had foreseen this and was beforehand with him. Even as his hand rose, the concussor struck the outer side of his arm, between the shoulder and the elbow, on the exact spot where the musculo-spiral nerve turns round the bone. The effect was most interesting. The sudden nerve stimulus produced an equally sudden contraction of the extensors. The forearm straightened with a jerk, the fingers shot out straight and the released revolver flew clattering along the hall floor.

"Anatomy has its uses even in a midnight scuffle.

"The suddenness of my appearance and the promptness of my action paralyzed him completely. He stared at me in abject terror and gibbered inarticulately. Only for a few moments, however. Then he turned and darted towards the street door.

"But I did not mean to let him escape. In a twinkling I was after him and had him by the collar. He uttered a savage snarl and dropped the lamp on the mat to free his hands; and, as the spring switch was released, the light went out, leaving us in total darkness. Now that he was at bay, he struggled furiously, and I could hear him snorting and cursing as he wriggled in my grasp. I had to drop the concussor that I might hold him with both hands, and it was well that I did, for he suddenly got one hand free and struck. It was a vicious blow and had it not been partly stopped by my elbow the adventure would have ended very differently, for I felt the point of a knife sweep across my chest, ripping open my pajama jacket and making a quite unpleasant little flesh-wound. On this I gripped him round the chest, pinioning both his arms as well as I could and trying to get possession of the knife, while he made frantic struggles to aim another blow.

"So, for awhile we remained locked in a deadly embrace, swaying to and fro, and each straining for the momentary advantage that would have brought the affair to a finish. The end came unexpectedly.

"One of us tripped on the edge of the mat and we both came down with a crash, he underneath and face downwards. As we fell, he uttered a sharp cry and began to struggle in a curious, convulsive fashion; but after a time he grew quieter and at last lay quite still and silent.

"At first I took this for a ruse to put me off my guard, and held on more firmly than ever; but presently a characteristic limpness of his limbs suggested a new idea. Gradually and cautiously I relaxed my hold, and, as he still did not move, I felt about on the mat for the lamp; and when I had found it and pushed over the switch I threw its light on him.

"He was perfectly motionless and did not appear to be breathing. I turned him over and then saw that it was as I had suspected. He had held the knife ready for a second blow when I had pinioned him. He was still grasping it so when we fell, and the point had entered his own chest near the middle line, between the

44

fourth and fifth ribs, and had been driven in up to the very haft by the force of the fall. He must have died almost instantaneously.

"I stood up and listened. The place was as silent as the grave; a remarkably apt comparison, by the way. The pistol shots had apparently not been heard by the police, so there was no fear of interruption from that quarter; and as for the maids they were very carefully keeping out of harm's way.

"Still, there was a good deal to do, and not so very much time to do it in. It was now getting on for three o'clock and the sun would be up by four. Daylight would bring the maids down and everything must be clear before they made their appearance.

"I wasted no time. One by one, I conveyed the bodies to the laboratory and deposited them in the tank, the accommodation of which was barely equal to the occasion. The sudden death of the first man had rather puzzled me, but when I lifted him the explanation was obvious enough. The heavy blow, catching the head obliquely, had dislocated the neck. So the concussor was not such a very harmless implement after all.

"The slight traces left in transporting the material to the laboratory, I obliterated with great care, excepting the last man's knife, which I left on the mat. Then I changed my pajamas, putting the blood-stained suit to soak in the laboratory, strapped up my wound, put on a dressing-gown, opened the street door and shut it rather noisily and ascended with a candle to the upper floor.

"The housemaid's bedroom door was open and the room empty. I tapped at the cook's door and elicited a faint scream.

"'Who's that?' a shaky voice demanded.

"'It is I,' was my answer—a stupid answer, by the way, but, of course, they knew my voice. The door opened and the two women appeared, fully dressed but rather disheveled and both very pale.

"'Is anything the matter, sir?' the housemaid asked.

"'Yes,' I replied. 'I think there has been a burglary. I woke in the night and thought I heard a pistol-shot, but, putting it down to a dream, I went to sleep again. Did either of you hear anything?'

"'I thought I heard a pistol go off, sir,' said the cook, 'and so did Susan. That's why she came in here.'

"'Ah!' said I, 'then it was not a dream. Then just now I

45

distinctly heard the street door shut, so I went down and found the gas alight in the dining-room and the safe open.'

"'Lor', sir!' exclaimed Susan, 'I hope nothing's been took.' (She spoke exceedingly badly for a good-class housemaid.)

"'That,' said I, 'is what I wish you to find out. Perhaps you will come down and take a look round. There is no one about now.'

"On this they came down with alacrity, each provided with a candle, all agog, no doubt, to see what success their friends had had. The first trace of the intruders was a large blood-stain at the foot of the stairs, at which Susan shied like a horse. There was another stain near the street door, and there was the burglar's knife on the mat, which the cook picked up and then dropped with a faint scream. I examined it and discovered the letters 'G.B.' cut on the handle.

"'It looks,' I remarked, 'as if the burglars had quarreled. However, that is none of our business. Let us see what has happened to the safe.'

"We went into the dining-room and the two women looked eagerly at the open safe; but though they both repeated the hope that 'nothing had been took,' they could hardly conceal their disappointment when they saw that the contents were intact. I examined the roughly-made false key without comment but with a significant glance at them which I think they understood; and I overhauled a couple of large carpet bags, neither of which contained anything but the outfit of appliances for the raid.

"'I suppose I ought to communicate with the police,' said I (without the slightest intention of doing anything of the kind).

"'I don't see what good that would do, sir,' said Susan. 'The men is gone and nothing hasn't been took. The police would only come in and turn the place upside down and take up your time for nothing.'

"Thus Susan Slodger, with a vivid consciousness of the false key, made exactly the suggestion that I desired. Of course it would never do to have the police in the house again so soon. I affected to be deeply impressed by her sagacity and in the end decided to 'let sleeping dogs lie.' Only Susan did not realize how exceedingly soundly they slept.

"It was necessary for me to visit the osteological dealer in the course of the morning to obtain three suitable skeletons as understudies according to my plan. This was quite indispensable. The dealer's receipt and invoice for three human skeletons was my passport of safety. But I regretted the necessity. For it was certain that as soon as I was out of the house one of these hussies would run off to make inquiries about her friends; and when it was found that the burglars were missing, there might be trouble. You can never calculate the actions of women. I did not suppose that either of them was capable of breaking into the laboratory. But still, one or both of them might. And if they did, the fat would be in the fire with a vengeance.

"However, it had to be done, and accordingly I set forth after breakfast with a spring tape and a note of the measurements in my pocket. Fortunately the dealer had just received a large consignment of skeletons from Germany (Heaven alone knows whence these German exporters obtain their supply), so I had an ample number to select from; and as they ran rather small—I suspect they were mostly Frenchmen—I had no difficulty in matching my specimens, which, as is usual with criminals, were all below the average stature.

"On my return I found that the housemaid was out, 'doing some shopping,' the cook explained. But she returned shortly, and as soon as I saw her I knew that she had been making 'kind inquiries.' Her manner was most peculiar, and so was the cook's for that matter. They were both profoundly depressed and anxious; they both regarded me with evident dislike and still more evident fear. They mumped about the house, silent and restless; they showed an inconvenient desire to keep me in sight and yet they hurried out of the rooms at my approach.

"The housemaid was very much disturbed. When waiting at table, she eyed me incessantly and if I moved suddenly she jumped. Once she dropped a soup tureen merely because I looked at her rather attentively; she was continually missing my wine-glass and pouring the claret on to the table-cloth; and when I tested the edge of a poultry-carver, which had become somewhat blunt, she

47

hurried from the room and I saw her watching me through the crack of the door.

"The arrival of the 'understudy' skeletons from the dealers a couple of days later gave her a terrible shock. I was in the dining-room when they arrived and through the open door heard what passed; and certainly the incident was not without a humorous side.

"The carrier came to the front door and to Susan, who answered his ring, he addressed himself with the familiarity of his class.

"'Here's three cases for your master. Funny uns, they are, too. He don't happen to be in the resurrection line, I suppose?'

"'I don't know what you mean,' Susan replied, sourly.

"'You will when you see the cases,' the man retorted. 'Three of 'em, there are. Big uns. Where will you have 'em?'

"Susan came to me for instructions and I directed that they should be taken through to the museum, the door of which I unlocked for the purpose.

"The appearance of the cases was undeniably funereal, not in shape only but also in color; for the dealer, with an ill-timed sense of fitness, had had them painted black. And the effect was heightened by the conduct of the two grinning carriers, who bore each case on their shoulders, coffin-wise, and proceeded to the museum at a slow, funereal walk; and when I was out of sight, though not out of earshot, I heard the leading carrier, who seemed to be somewhat of a humorist, softly whistling the 'Dead March in Saul.'

"Meanwhile, Susan Slodger stood in the hall with a face as white as a tallow candle. She stared with fearful fascination at the long, black cases and uttered no sound even when the facetious carrier questioned her as to the destination of 'our dear departed brother.' She was absolutely thunderstruck.

"When the carriers had gone I directed her to come to the museum and help me to unpack the cases, which she flatly refused to do unless supported by the cook. To this, of course, I had no objection, and when she went off to the kitchen to fetch her colleague, I took up a position just inside the laboratory door and awaited developments. The cases had hinged lids secured with a simple hook, so that when the binding cords were cut there would be no difficulty in ascertaining the nature of the contents.

"The two women came briskly through the lobby, the cook babbling cheerfully and the housemaid silent; but at the museum door they both stopped short and the former ejaculated, 'Gawd! what's this?'

"Here I stepped out and explained, 'These are some cases of specimens for the museum. I want you to unfasten the cords. That is all. I will take out the things myself.' With this I went back to the laboratory; but in less than half a minute I heard a series of shrieks, and the two women raced through the lobby and disappeared below stairs.

"After this the position grew worse than ever. Though obviously terrified of me, these two women dogged me incessantly. It was most inconvenient, for the excess of material kept me exceedingly busy; and to make things worse, I had received from Jamrach's (without an order—but I had to keep the thing) a dead hyena which had been affected with osteitis deformans. It was a fine specimen and was useful as serving to explain my great preoccupation; but it added to my labors and made me impatient of interruptions.

"The museum wing had an entrance of its own in a side street for the delivery of material (such as the hyena), and this gave me some relief; for I could go out of the front door and slip in by the side entrance. But Susan soon discovered this and thereafter was continually banging at the lobby door to see if I was in. I don't know what she thought. She was an ignorant woman and stupid, but I think she vaguely associated my labors in the laboratory with her absent friends.

"This perpetual spying on my actions became at last intolerable and I was on the point of sending the two hussies about their business when an accident put an end to the state of affairs. I had gone out of the front door and let myself in by the side entrance, but, by some amazing inadvertence, had left the lobby door unfastened; and I had barely got on my apron to begin work when I heard someone enter the lobby. Then came a gentle tapping at the door of the laboratory. I took no notice, but waited to see what would happen. The tapping was repeated louder and yet louder, and still I made no move. Then, after an interval, I heard a wire inserted in the lock.

"I determined to make an end of this. Quietly concealing the material on which I was working, I took down from a hook a large butterfly-net (my poor wife had been interested in Lepidoptera). Very softly I tip-toed to the door and suddenly flung it open. There stood Susan Slodger with a hair-pin in her hand, absolutely paralyzed with terror. In a moment, before she had time to recover, I had slipped the butterfly-net over her head.

"That revived her. With a piercing yell she turned and fled, and with such precipitancy that she pulled the net off the handle. I saw her flying down the lobby with the net over her head, looking like an oriental bride; I heard the street door bang, and I found the butter-fly net on the doormat. But Susan Slodger I never set eyes on again.

"The cook left me the same day, taking Susan's box with her. It was a great relief. I now had the house to myself and could work without interruption or the discomfort of being spied upon. As to the products of my labors, they are fully set forth in the catalogue; and of this adventure I can only say to the visitor to my museum in the words of the well-known inscription, 'Si monumentum requiris, circumspice'."

Such was Challoner's account of his acquisition of the specimens numbered 2, 3 and 4. The descriptions of the preparations were, as he had said, set out in dry and precise detail in the catalogue, and some of the particulars were really quite interesting, as, for instance, the fact that "the skull of Number 4 combines an extreme degree of dolichocephaly (67.5) with a cranial capacity of no more than 1523 cubic centimeters." It was certainly what one might have expected from his conduct.

But to the general reader the question which will suggest itself is, What was the state of Challoner's mind? Was he mad? Was he wicked? Or had he merely an unconventional point of view? It is to the latter opinion that I incline after long consideration. He clearly rejected the criminal as a fellow-creature and regarded

50

himself as a public benefactor in eliminating him. And perhaps he was right.

As to the apparently insane pleasure that he took in the actual captures, I can only say that sane men take a pleasure in the slaughter of harmless animals—such as the giraffe—for which they have no need; and other sane men actually go abroad and kill—by barbarous methods—foreign men of estimable character with whom they have no quarrel. This sport they call war and seem to enjoy it. But killing is killing; and a foreign peasant's life is surely worth more than a British criminal's.

This, however, is only an obiter dictum from which many will no doubt dissent.

IV

THE GIFTS OF CHANCE

The testamentary arrangements of eccentric people must, from time to time, have put their legatees in possession of some very queer property. I call to mind an old gentleman who bequeathed to a distant relative the products of a lifetime of indiscrimate collecting; which products included an obsolete field gun, a stuffed camel, a collection of bottled tapeworms, a fire engine, a church pulpit and the internal fittings of a public-house bar. And other instances could be quoted. But surely no legatee ever found himself in possession of a queerer legacy than that which my poor friend Challoner had bequeathed to me when he made over to me the mortal remains of some two dozen deceased criminals.

The bequest would have been an odd one under any circumstances, but what made it much more so was the strange intimacy that became established between me and the deceased. To the ordinary observer a skeleton in a museum case or in an art school conveys no vivid sense of humanity. That this bony shape was once an actual person, a Me, that walked abroad and wore clothes, that loved and hated, sorrowed and rejoiced, that had friends and lovers, parents and perhaps children; that was, in short, a living man or woman, occurs to him but vaguely. The thing is an osteological specimen; a mere anatomical abstraction.

Now these skeletons of Challoner's were quite different. Walking down the long room and looking into the great wall-case, I was confronted with actual individuals. Number One was Jimmy Archer, who had tried to steal the "blimy teapot." Number Three was the burglar Fred; I could tell him by the notch on his fifth rib that his comrade's bullet had made. Number Two was the man who had fired that shot, and Number Four was Joe, who was "done in in the dark." I knew them all. The weird "Museum Archives" had told me all about them; and as to the rest of that grisly company, strangers to me as yet, the neatly written, Russia-bound volume that Challoner had left would give me their histories too.

It was some days before I was able to resume my reading of the uncanny little book, but an unoccupied evening at length gave me the opportunity. As ten o'clock struck, I put on my slippers, adjusted the light, drew an armchair up to my study fire and opened the volume at the place marked by the envelope that I had inserted at the end of the last reading. The page was headed "Circumstances attending the acquirement of Numbers Five and Six," and the account ran as follows:

"The most carefully conceived plans, when put into practice, are apt to discover unforeseen defects. My elaborate plan for the capture of burglars was no exception to the rule. The idea of employing palpably dishonest servants to act as decoy ducks to lure the burglars on to the premises was an excellent one and had fully answered my expectations. But it had a defect which I had overlooked. The burglars themselves, when reduced to a condition suitable for exhibition in a show-case, were entirely innocuous. There was no danger of their making any indiscreet statements. But with the servants—female servants, too—it was quite otherwise. From the shelter of my roof they had gone forth to sow distrust and suspicion in quarters where perfect confidence and trustfulness should prevail. It was a most unfortunate oversight. Now, when it was too late, I saw clearly that they ought never to have left me. I ought to have added them to the collection, too.

"The evil results of the mistake soon became apparent. I had replaced the late cook and housemaid by two women of quite unimpeachable dishonesty, of whom I had, naturally, great hopes. But nothing happened. I let them handle the plate freely, I gave them the key of the safe from time to time, I brushed the sham diamond pendants and bracelets under their very noses, and still there was no result. It is true that the silver spoons dwindled in number and that a stray candlestick or salt-cellar would now and again 'report absent'; that the tradesmen's bills were preposterous and that the tea consumed in a week would have impaired the digestion of a Lodge of Good Templars. But that was all. No aspirant for museum honors made his appearance. The concussor

53

became dusty with disuse; the safe in the dining-room remained neglected and untouched, and as for the burglar alarm, I had to stand on it myself at stated intervals to keep it in working order.

"I had already resolved to get rid of those two women when they saved me the trouble. I directed them to accompany me to the laboratory to clean out the furnace, whereat they both turned pale and flatly refused; and I saw them half an hour later secretly handing their boxes up the area steps to a man with a barrow. Obviously someone had told them something of my methods.

"The cook and housemaid who succeeded them were jail-birds pure and simple. They were dirty, dishonest, lazy and occasionally drunk. But for their actual function they were quite useless. They drank my whiskey, they devoured and distributed my provisions, they stole my portable property, and once, when I had incautiously left the door unfastened, I caught them browsing round the museum; but they brought no grist to my mill.

"It is true that during their reign I had one visitor, a scurvy little wry-faced knave who sneaked in through the scullery window; but I think he had no connection with them or he would have entered by some more convenient route and have used a false key instead of a jimmy to open the safe. He was a wretched little creature and his capture quite uninteresting; for, when he had bitten me twice, he crumpled up like a rag doll and I carried him to the tank as if he had been a monkey.

"Yet I ought not to disparage him unduly, for he was the one specimen in my collection, up to that time, who presented the orthodox 'stigmata of degeneration.' His hair was bushy, his face strikingly asymmetrical, and his ears were like a pair of Lombroso's selected examples; outstanding, with enormous Darwinian tubercles and almost devoid of lobules.

"Still, whatever his points of interest, he was but a stray catch. Chance had brought him as it might bring others of the same kind in the course of years. But this would not answer my purpose. Numbers were what I wanted and what I had arranged for; and it was with deep disappointment that I recognized that my plan had failed. The supply of anthropological material had come to an end. In a word, the criminal class had 'smoked' me.

54

"This was not mere surmise on my part. I had direct and very quaint evidence of it soon after I had completed the preparation of Number Five. I was returning home one evening and was approaching the vicinity of my house when I became aware of a small man of seedy aspect who appeared to be following me. I slackened my pace somewhat to let him overtake or pass me, and when nearly opposite my side door (the museum entrance) he edged alongside and addressed me in a hoarse whisper.

"'Guv'nor.'

"I halted and looked at him attentively; a proceeding that caused him evident discomfort. 'Did you speak to me?' I asked.

"He edged up closer, but still did not meet my eye, and, looking first over one shoulder and then over the other, replied, 'Yus, I did, guv'nor.'

"'What do you want?' I demanded.

"He edged up yet closer and said in a hoarse undertone, 'I want to know what you've been and done with my cousin Bill.'

"'Your cousin Bill,' I repeated. 'Do I know him?'

"'I dunno whether you know 'im,' was the reply, 'but I see 'im go into your house and I never see 'im come out agin, and I want to know what you've been and done with 'im.'

"Now here was an interesting circumstance. I had already noted something familiar in the man's face. His question explained it. Cousin Bill was clearly Number Five in the Anthropological Series. In fact, the resemblance was quite remarkable. The present example, like the late Bill, was an undergrown creature, and had the same curiously-twisted nose, the same asymmetrical face and similar ears—large, flat ears that stood out from his head like the handles of an amphora, that had strongly marked Darwinian tubercles, unformed helices and undeveloped lobules. Lombroso would have loved him. He would have made a delightful photograph for purposes of illustration, and—it suddenly occurred to me—he would make a most interesting companion preparation to Number Five.

"'Your Cousin Bill,' I said, with this new idea in my mind. 'Was he the son of your mother's sister?' (A few details as to

55

heredity add materially to the value and instructiveness of a specimen.)

"'And supposin' he was. What about it? I want to know what you've been and done with 'im.'

"'What makes you think I have done anything with him?' I asked.

"'Why, I see 'im go into your 'ouse and I never see 'im come out.'

"'But, my good man,' I protested, 'that is exceedingly bad logic. If you saw him go in, there is a fair presumption that he went in—'

"'I see 'im with my own eyes,' my friend interrupted, as though there were other alternative means of vision.

"'But,' I continued, 'the fact that you did not see him come out establishes no presumption that he did not come out. He may have come out unobserved.'

"'No, he didn't. He never come out. I see 'im go in—'

"'So you have mentioned. May I ask what his business was?'

"'His business,' my acquaintance replied with some hesitation, 'was of a private nature.'

"'I see. Did he go in by the front door?'

"'No, 'e didn't. 'E went in by the scullery window.'

"'In the evening, no doubt?'

"'Two hay hem,' was the reply.

"'Ah!' said I. 'He went in by the scullery window at two A.M. on private business. Quite so! Well, you see, the common sense of the position is that if he went into the house and never came out, he must be in the house still."

"'That's just what I think,' my friend agreed.

"'Very well. Then in that case perhaps you would like to step in and look round to see if you can find him.' I took out my latch-key and motioned invitingly towards the museum door.

"'No yer don't,' exclaimed the man, backing away hastily down the street. 'Yer don't git me in there, so I tell yer straight.'

"'What do you want me to do, then?'

"'I want to know,' he reiterated, 'what you've been and done with my cousin Bill. I see 'im go into—'

"'I know,' I interrupted impatiently. 'You said that before.'

"'And look 'ere, guv'nor,' he added. 'Where did you git all them skillintons from?' Evidently somebody had been talking to this little rascal.

"'I can't go into questions of that kind, you know,' I replied.

"'No, I don't suppose yer can,' he retorted; 'but I'll tell yer what I think you've been and done with Bill. You got 'im in there and you done 'im in. That's what I think. And I tell yer it ain't the cheese. When a cove goes into an 'ouse for to do an 'armless crack he stands for to be lagged if so be as he 'appens to git copped. But 'e don't stand for to be done in. 'Tain't playin' the game, and I ain't a-goin' to 'ave it.'

"'Then what do you propose to do?' I asked with some curiosity.

"'I perpose,' the little wastrel replied haughtily, 'for to 'ave the loar on yer. I'm a-goin' to put the coppers on to this 'ere job.'

"With this he turned somewhat hastily and shambled away up the street at the quick shuffle characteristic of his class. I let myself in at the side door and proceeded to the museum to examine Number Five with renewed interest. The resemblance was remarkable. It was plainly traceable even in the skull and in the proportions of the skeleton generally, while in the small, dry preparation of the head the likeness was ridiculous. It was most regrettable that he should have refused my invitation to come in. As a companion preparation, illustrating the physical resemblances in degenerate families, he would have been invaluable.

"His conversation and his ludicrous threat of legal proceedings gave me much matter for reflection. To him burglary presented itself as a legitimate sporting pursuit governed by certain rules. The players were respectively the burglar and the householder, of whom the latter staked his property and the former a certain period of personal liberty; and the rules of the game were equally binding on both. It was a conception worthy of comic opera; and yet, incredible as it may seem, it is the very view of crime that is today accepted and acted upon by society.

"The threat uttered by my diminutive acquaintance had the sound of broad farce, and so, I may confess, I regarded it. The idea

57

of a burglar proceeding against a householder for hindering him in the execution of his private business might have emanated from the whimsical brain of the late W.S. Gilbert. The quaint topsy-turveydom of it caused me many a chuckle of amusement when I recalled the interview during the next few days; but, of course, I never dreamed of any actual attempt to carry out the threat.

"Imagine, therefore, my astonishment when I realized that not only had the complaint been made, but the law had actually been set—at least tentatively—in motion.

"The stunning discovery descended on me with the force of a concussor three days after the interview with Number Five's cousin. I was sitting in my study reading Chevers' 'Crime against the Person' when the housemaid entered with a visiting card. 'A gentleman wished to see me to discuss certain scientific matters with me.'

"I looked at the card. It bore the name of 'Mr. James Ramchild,' a name quite unknown to me. It was very odd. A scientific colleague would surely have written for an appointment and stated the object of his visit. I looked at the card again. It was printed from script type instead of the usual engraved plate and it bore an address in Kennington Park Road. These were weighty facts and a trifle suspicious. I seemed to scent a traveler from beyond the Atlantic; a traveler of commercial leanings.

"'Show Mr. Ramchild up here,' I said, and the housemaid departed, to return anon accompanied by a tall, massive man of a somewhat military aspect.

"I could have laughed aloud, but I did not. It would not have been politic and it would certainly not have been polite. But I chuckled inwardly as I offered my visitor a chair. 'Experientia docet!' I had seen quite a number of plain-clothes police officers in the last few months and the present specimen would have been typical even without his boots. I prepared to enjoy myself.

"'I have taken the liberty of calling on you, Mr. Challoner,' my visitor began, 'to make a few enquiries concerning—er—skeletons.'

"'I nodded gravely and smothered a giggle. He was a simple soul, this Ramchild. 'Concerning skeletons!' What an expression for a man of science to use! An artless creature indeed! A veritable Ramchild of nature, so to speak.

"'I understand,' he continued, 'that you have a famous collection of—er—skeletons.' I nodded again. Of course I had not anything of the kind. Mine was only a little private collection. But it was of no consequence. 'So,' he concluded, 'I have called to ask if you would be so kind as to let me see them.'

"'From whom did you hear of my collection?' I asked.

"'It was mentioned to me by my friend Mr.—er—Mr. Winterbottom, of Cambridge.'

"'Ah,' said I, 'I remember Winterbottom very well. How is he?'

"'He's very well, thank you,' replied the detective, looking mightily surprised; and not without reason, seeing that he had undoubtedly invented the name Winterbottom on the spur of the moment.

"'Is there any branch of the subject that you are especially interested in?' I asked, purposely avoiding giving him a lead.

"'No,' he replied. 'No, not particularly. The fact is that I thought of starting a collection myself if it wouldn't be too expensive. But you have a regular museum, haven't you?'

"'Yes. Come and have a look at it.'

"He rose with alacrity and I led him through the dining-room to the museum wing, and I noticed that, if he did not know much about osteology, he was uncommonly observant of the details of house-construction. He looked very hard at the safe, the mahogany casing of which failed to disguise its nature from the professional eye, and noted the massive door that gave entrance to the museum wing and the Yale lock that secured it. In the museum his eye riveted itself on the five human skeletons in the great wall-case, but I perversely led him to the case containing my curious collection of abnormal and deformed skeletons of the lower animals.

"'There,' I said complacently, 'that is my little hoard. Is there any specimen that you would like to take out and examine?'

"He gazed vaguely into the case and murmured that 'they were all very interesting,' and again I caught his eye wandering to the great case opposite. I was in the act of reaching out a porcupine

59

with an ankylosed knee-joint, when he plucked up courage to say frankly, 'The fact is, I am principally interested in human skeletons.'

"I replaced the porcupine and walked across to the great wall-case. 'I am sorry I have not more to show you,' I said apologetically. 'This is only the beginning of a collection, you see; but still, the specimens are of considerable interest. Don't you find them so?'

"Apparently he did, for he scrutinized the dates on the dwarf-pedestals with the deepest attention and finally remarked, 'I see you have written a date on each of these. What does that signify?'

"'The dates are those on which I acquired the respective specimens,' I answered.

"'Oh, indeed.' He reflected, with a profoundly speculative eye on Number Five. I judged that he was trying to recall a date furnished by Number Five's cousin and that he would have liked to consult his note-book.

"'The particulars,' I said, 'are too lengthy to put on the labels, but they are set out in detail in the catalogue.'

"'Can I see the catalogue?' he asked eagerly.

"'Certainly.' I produced a small manuscript volume—not the catalogue which is attached to the 'Archives,' but a dummy that I had prepared for such a contingency as had arisen—and handed it to him. He opened it with avidity, and, turning at once to Number Five, began, with manifest disappointment, to read the description aloud.

"'5. Male skeleton of Teutonic type exhibiting well-marked characters of degeneration. The skull is asymmetrical, subdolichocephalic.' (He pronounced this word subdolichocolophalic' and paused abruptly, turning rather red. It is an awkward word.) 'Yes,' he said, closing the catalogue, 'very interesting, very remarkable. Exceedingly so. I should very much like to possess a skeleton like that.'

"'You are much better off with the one you have got,' I remarked.

"'Oh, I don't mean that,' he rejoined hastily. 'I mean that I should like to acquire a specimen like this Number Five for my proposed collection. Now how could I get one?'

"'Well,' I said reflectively, 'there are several ways.' I paused and he gazed at me expectantly. 'You could, for instance,' I continued slowly, 'provide yourself with a lasso and take a walk down Whitechapel High Street.'

"'Good gracious!' he exclaimed excitedly; 'do you really mean to say that—'

"'Certainly,' I interrupted. 'You would find an abundance of material. For my own part, not being gifted with your exceptionally fine physique, I have to adopt the more prosaic and expensive plan of buying my specimens from the dealers.'

"'Quite so, quite so,' he agreed. He was deeply disappointed and inclined to be huffy. 'Of course you were joking about the lasso. But would you mind giving me the address of the dealer from whom you obtained this specimen?' And once more he pointed to Cousin Bill.

"He thought he had cornered me; and so he would have done if I had been less cautious. I congratulated myself on the wisdom and foresight that had led me to provide myself with those dummy skeletons. For now I held him in the hollow of my hand.

"'That specimen?' I said, scanning the date on the pedestal; 'I fancy I got it from Hammerstein. You know his place in the Seven Dials, no doubt. A very useful man. I get most of my human osteology from him.' I fetched my receipt file and turned over the papers in leisurely fashion while he gnawed his lips with impatience. At last I found the receipted invoice and he read it aloud with a ludicrous expression of disappointment.

"'Complete set superfine human osteology strongly articulated with best brass wire and screw-bolts, with springs to mandible and stout iron supporting rod. All bones guaranteed to be derived from the same subject. £5.3.4.'

"The invoice was headed, 'Oscar Hammerstein, Dealer in Osteology, Great St. Andrew Street, London, W.C.,' and was dated 4th February, 1891.

"The detective entered the name and address in a black-bound note-book of official aspect, compared the date with that on Cousin Bill's pedestal and prepared to depart.

"'There is one thing I must point out to you,' I said, anticipating an early visit on my friend's part to Mr. Hammerstein;

'the skeletons as you get them from the dealers are not always up to museum style in point of finish. They are often of a bad color and may be stained with grease. If they are, you will have to disarticulate them, clean them with benzol and, if necessary, remacerate and bleach; but whatever you do,' I concluded solemnly, 'be careful with the chlorinated soda or you will spoil the appearance of the bones and make them brittle. Good bye!' I shook his hand effusively and he took his departure very glum and crestfallen.

"As long as he had been with me, something of the old buoyant spirit of playfulness—that was my ordinary mood until my great trouble befell—had been revived by the absurdity of the situation. But his departure left me rather depressed, for his visit marked the final collapse of my scheme. Even if the criminal classes had been willing to continue the supply of anthropological material, my methods could not have been carried out under the watchful and disapproving eyes of the police.

"What then was to be done? This was the question that I asked myself again and again. As to abandoning my activities, of course, such an idea never occurred to me. I remained alive for a definite purpose: to search for the man who had murdered my wife and to exact from him payment of his debt. Of this purpose, the collection had been, at first, a mere by-product; and though it was gradually taking such hold of me as to become a purpose in itself, it was but a minor purpose. The discovery of that unknown wretch was the Mecca of my earthly pilgrimage, from which no difficulties or obstacles should divert me.

"The hint that ultimately guided me into new fields of research came to me by the merest chance. A few days after the visit of the detective I received a letter from one of my few remaining friends, a Dr. Grayson, who had formerly practiced in London as a physician, but who, owing to age and infirmity, had retired to his native place, the village of Shome, near Rochester. Grayson asked me to spend a day with him, that we might talk over some matters in which we were both interested; and, being now rather at a loose end, I accepted the invitation, but declined to sleep away from home and my collection.

"It is significant of my state of mind at this time that, before starting, I considered what weapon I should take with me. Formerly I should no more have thought of arming myself for a simple railway journey than of putting on a coat of mail; but now a train suggested a train robber—a Lefroy, with a very unsubmissive Mr. Gold—and the long tunnel near Strood was but the setting of a railway tragedy. My ultimate choice of weapon, too, is interesting. The familiar revolver I rejected utterly. There must be no noise. My quarrel with the criminal was a personal one in which no outsiders must be allowed to meddle. I should have preferred the concussor, which I now handled with skill, but it was hardly a portable tool, and my choice ultimately fell on a very fine swordstick, supplemented by a knuckle-duster which had been bequeathed to me by one of my clients after trial on my own countenance.

"And after all, nothing happened. I got into an empty first-class compartment and when, just as the train was starting, a burly fellow dashed in and slammed the door, I eyed him suspiciously and waited for developments. But there were none. The fellow sat huddled in a corner, watching me and keeping an eye on the handle of the alarm over his head; but he made no sign. When we emerged from the long tunnel he was as white as a ghost and he hopped out on to Strood platform almost before the train had begun to slow down.

"I reached my bag down from the rack and got out after him, smiling at my own folly. The criminal was becoming an obsession of which I must beware if I would not end my days in an asylum; a fact which was further impressed on me when I saw my late fellow-passenger, who had just caught sight of me, 'legging it' down the station approach like a professional pedestrian and looking back nervously over his shoulder. Resolving firmly to put the subject out of my mind, I walked slowly into the town and betook myself to the London Road; and though, as I passed the Falstaff Inn and crossed Gad's Hill, fleeting reminiscences of Prince Henry and the men in buckram came unsought, with later suggestions of a stagecoach struggling up the hill in the dark and masked figures creeping down the banks into the sunken road, I kept to my good resolution. The bag was a little cumbersome—it contained a large parcel of

63

bulbs from Covent Garden that Grayson had asked me to bring—and yet it was pleasant to break off from the high road and stray by well-remembered tracks and footpaths across the fields. It was all familiar ground; for in years gone by, when Grayson was in practice, we would come down together for weekends to his little demesne, and often I would stay on alone for a week or so and ramble about the country by myself. So I knew every inch of the country side and was so much interested in renewing my acquaintance with it that I was twenty minutes late for lunch.

"I had a most agreeable day with Grayson (who was working at the historical aspects of disease), and would have stayed later than I did. But at about half-past eight—we had dined at seven—Grayson began to be restless and fidgetty and at last said apologetically:

"'Don't think me inhospitable, Challoner, but if you aren't going to stay the night you had better be going. And don't go by Gad's Hill. Take the road down to Higham and catch the train there.'

"'Why, what is the matter with Gad's Hill?' I asked.

"'Nothing much by daylight, but a great deal at night. It has always been an unsafe spot and is especially just now. There has been quite an epidemic of highway robberies lately. They began when the hoppers were here last autumn, but some of those East-end ruffians seem to have settled in the neighborhood. I have seen some very queer-looking characters even in this village; aliens, apparently, of the kind that you see about Stepney and Whitechapel.

"'Now, you get down to Higham, like a good fellow, before the country settles down for the night.'

"Needless to say, the prowling alien had no terrors for me, but as Grayson was really uneasy, I made no demur and took my leave almost immediately. But I did not make directly for Higham. The moon was up and the village looked very inviting. Tree and chimney-stack, thatched roof and gable-end cut pleasant shapes of black against the clear sky, and patches of silvery light fell athwart the road on wooden palings and weather-boarded fronts. I strolled along the little street, carrying the now light and empty bag and exchanging greetings with scattered villagers, until I came to the lane that turns down towards the London Road. Here, by a triangular patch of green, I halted and mechanically looked at my watch, holding it up in the moonlight. I was about to replace it when a voice asked:

"'What's the right time, mister?'

"I looked up sharply. The man who had spoken was sitting on the bank under the hedge and in such deep shadow that I had not noticed him. Nor could I see much of him now, though I observed that he seemed to be taking some kind of refreshment; but the voice was not a Kentish voice, nor even an English one; it seemed to engraft an unfamiliar, guttural accent on the dialect of East London.

"I told the man the time and asked him if the road—pointing to the ridgway—would take me to Higham. Of course I knew it would not and I have no very distinct idea why I asked. But he answered promptly enough, 'Yus. Straight down the road. Was you wantin' to get to the station?'

"I replied that I was, and he added, 'You go straight down the road a mile and a half and you'll see the station right in front of you.'

"Now, here was a palpable misdirection. Obviously intentional, too, for the circumstantiality excluded the idea of a mistake. He was deliberately sending me—an ostensible stranger— along a solitary side-road that led into the heart of the country. With what object? I had very little doubt, and that doubt should soon be set at rest.

"I thanked him for his information and set out along the road at an easy pace; but when I had gone a little way, I lengthened my stride so as to increase my speed without altering the rhythm of my footfalls. As I went, I speculated on the intentions of my friend and noted with interest and a little surprise that I was quite without fear of him. I suspected him of being a footpad, one of the gang of which Grayson had spoken, and I had set forth along this unfrequented road in a spirit of mere curiosity to see if it were really so.

"Presently I came to a gate at the entrance of a cart-track and here I halted to listen. From the road behind me came the sound of footsteps; quick steps but not sharp and crisp; rather of a shuffling, stealthy quality. I climbed quietly over the gate and took up a position behind the trunk of an elm that grew in the hedgerow. The footsteps came on apace. Soon round a bend of the moon-lighted road a figure appeared moving forward rapidly and keeping in what shadow there was. I watched it through the thick hedge as it approached and resolved itself into a seedy-looking man carrying a thick knobbed stick.

"Opposite the gate the man halted and, as I could see by his shadow, looked across the silvery fields that stretched away down to the valley and listened, but only for a few moments. Then he started forward again at something between a quick walk and a slow trot.

"As soon as he had gone I came out and began to walk down the cart-track. My figure must have stood out conspicuously on the bare field and must have been plainly visible from the ridge-way. I did not hurry. Pursuing my way quietly down the gentle slope, I went on for some three hundred yards until the ground fell away more steeply; and here, before descending, I looked over my shoulder.

"A man was getting over the gate.

"I walked on more quickly now until I topped a second rise and then I again looked back. The figure of the man stood out on the brow of the hill, black against the moonlit sky. And now he was hurrying forward in undisguised pursuit.

"I quickened my pace and looked about me. The night was calm and lovely, the fields bathed in silvery light and the wooded uplands shrouded in a soft, gray shadow, from the heart of which a single lighted window gleamed forth, a spot of rosy warmth. The bark of a watch-dog came softened by distance from some solitary farmstead, and far away below, the hoot of a steamer, creeping up the river to the twinkling anchorage.

"Presently I came to a spot where the rough road divided. One well-worn track led down towards the footpath that ultimately enters the London Road; a fainter track led, as I knew, to an old chalk-pit where, in mysterious caverns, the farm carts rested through the winter months. Here I halted for a moment as if in doubt. The man was now less than a hundred yards behind me and walking as fast as he could. I turned round and looked at him, he appeared once more to hesitate, and then started at a run along the track to the chalk-pit.

"There was no disguise about the man's intentions. As I started off, he broke into a run and followed, but he did not hail me to stop. I suppose he knew whither the path led. But if his purpose was definite, so was mine. And again I noted with faint surprise that I had no feeling of nervousness. My contact with the criminal class had left me with nothing but a sentiment of hostile contempt. That a criminal might kill me never presented itself as a practical possibility. I was only concerned in inducing him to give me a fair pretext for killing him. So I ran on, wondering if my pursuer had ringed hair; if it were possible that, in this remote place and by this chance meeting, I might find the object of my quest; and conscious of that fierce, playful delight that always came over me when I was hunting the enemies of my race. For, of course, I was now hunting the fellow behind me, although the poor devil supposed he was hunting me.

"When the track approached the chalk-pit, it descended rather suddenly. I ran down between two clumps of bushes, into the weed-grown area at the bottom, past the row of caverns wherein the wagons were even now lurking unseen, and on until the track ended among a range of mole-hills in a sort of bay encompassed by the time-stained cliff. Here I wheeled about, putting down my bag, and faced my pursuer.

"'Stand off!' I said sharply. 'What are you following me for?'

"The man stopped and then approached more slowly. 'Look 'ere, mister,' said he, 'I don't want to hurt yer. You needn't be afeared of me.'

"'Well,' said I, 'What do you want?'

"'I'll tell yer,' he said confidentially. 'I'm a pore man, I am; I ain't got no watch, I ain't got no money and I can't get no work. Now you're a rich man. You've got a very 'andsome watch—I see it—and lots more at 'ome, I dessay. Well, you makes me a present o' that watch, that's what you do; and any small change that you've got about yer. You do that and I'll let yer go peaceable.'

"'And supposing I don't?'

"'Then some o' them farm blokes 'ill find a dead man in a chalk-pit. And it ain't no good for you to holler. There ain't no one within a mile of this place. So you pass over that watch and turn out yer bloomin' pockets.'

"'Do I understand—' I began; but he interrupted me savagely:

"'Oh, shut yer face and hand over! D'yer hear?' He advanced threateningly, grasping his bludgeon by the smaller end, but when he had approached within a couple of paces I made a sudden lunge with my stick, introducing its ferrule to his abdomen about the region of the solar plexus. He sprang back with an astonished yelp—which sounded like 'Ow—er!'—and stood gasping and rubbing his abdomen. As he recovered, he broke out into absurd and disgusting speech and began cautiously to circle round me, balancing his club in readiness for a smashing blow.

"'You wait till I done with yer,' said he, watching for a chance. 'I'll make yer pay for that. I'm a-goin' to do yer in, I am. You'll look ugly when I've finished—Ow—er!' The concluding exclamation was occasioned by the ferrule of my stick impinging on the fleshy part of his chest, and as he uttered it he sprang back out of range.

"After this he kept a greater distance, but continued to circle round and pour out an unceasing torrent of foul words. But he had not the faintest idea how to use a stick, whereas my practice with the foils at the gymnasium had made me quite skilful. From time to time he raised his bludgeon and ran in at me, but a sharp prod under the upraised arm always sent him leaping back out of reach with the inevitable 'Ow—er!'

"His lack of skill deprived the encounter of much of its interest. I think he felt this himself, for I saw him looking about furtively as if in search of something. Then he espied a large and knobbly flint and would have picked it up; but as he was stooping I plied the point of my stick so vigorously that he staggered back with yelps of pain.

"And now it was suddenly borne in upon me that he had had enough. I realized it just in time to plant myself on the track between him and the entrance to the chalk-pit. He was still as savage and murderous as ever, but his nerve was gone. He shrank away from me and as I followed closely he tried again and again to dodge past towards the opening.

"'Look 'ere, mister,' he said at length, 'you chuck it and I'll let yer go peaceable.'

"Let me go! I laughed scornfully, but stood my ground. And yet it was unpleasant. One cannot go on hammering a beaten man and it is difficult to refuse a surrender. On the other hand, it was out of the question to let this fellow go. He had come here prepared to murder me for a paltry watch and a handful of loose change. Common justice and my duty to my fellow men demanded his elimination. Besides, if I let him escape into the open, what would happen? The fields were sprinkled with big flints. It was practically certain that I should never leave the neighborhood alive.

"Even as I stood hesitating, he furnished an illustrative commentary on my thoughts. Springing back from me, he suddenly stooped and caught up a great flint nodule; and though I ducked quickly as he flung it and so avoided its full force, I caught such a buffet as it glanced off the side of my head as convinced me that a settlement must be speedily arrived at. Rushing in on him, I bore him backwards until he was penned up in the entrance of one of the caverns against the shafts of a wagon. Then suddenly he changed his tactics. Realizing at last that a clumsily-wielded bludgeon is powerless against a stick expertly handled rapier-wise, he dropped his club, and the next moment the moonbeams flashed from the broad blade of a knife. This was quite a different affair. He now stood on guard with the knife poised and his left hand outspread ready to snatch at my stick. It was a much more effective plan; only he did not know that inside my stout malacca reposed a keen Toledo sword-blade.

"I slipped my thumb on the press-button of the sword-stick and watched him. From time to time he made a dash at me with his knife, and when I prodded him back, he snatched at the stick. Again and again he nearly caught it, but I was just a little too quick for him, and he fell back, gasping and cursing, on the wagon-shafts. And then the end came with inevitable suddenness. He rushed out on me with upraised knife. I stopped him with a vigorous poke in the chest; but before I could whisk away the stick he had clutched it

69

with a howl of joy. I gave a final drive, pressed the button and sprang back, leaving the scabbard-end in his hand. Before he had realized what had happened, he darted out, brandishing the knife, and came fairly on the point of the sword-blade. At the same moment I must have lunged, though I was not aware of it, for when he staggered back the handle was against his breast.

"It was over, and I had hardly realized that the final stage had begun. In an instant, as it seemed, that yelping, murderous wretch had subsided into a huddled, inert heap. It was a quick and merciful dispatch. By the time I had cleaned the blade and replaced it in its scabbard, the last twitchings had ceased. As I stood and looked down at him, I felt something of the chill of an anticlimax. It had all gone off so easily.

"Now that it was finished, my thoughts went back to the final purpose of my quest. Was this man, by any chance, the wretch whom I was seeking? It did not seem likely, and yet the possibility must be considered. The first question was as to his hair. Stooping down, with my pocket scissors I cut off a good-sized lock and secured it in an envelope for future examination. Then, taking out my pocket-book, I pressed his fingers on some of the blank leaves. The natural surface of his hands offered a passable substitute for ink and the finger-prints could be further developed at home.

"Then arose a more difficult question. I naturally wished to add him to my collection; but the thing seemed impossible. I certainly could not take him away with me. But if I left him exposed, he would undoubtedly be found and buried and thus an excellent specimen would be lost to science. There was only one thing to be done. The middle of the chalk-pit was occupied by a large area covered with nettles and other large weeds. Probably no human being trod on that space from one year's end to another, for the stinging-nettles, four or five feet high, were enough to keep off stray children. Even now the spring vegetation was coming up apace. If I placed the body inconspicuously in the middle of the weedy area it would soon be overgrown and hidden. Then the natural agencies would do the rougher part of my work. Necrophagous insects and other vermin would come to the aid of air, moisture and bacteria, and I could return in the autumn and gather up the bones all ready for the museum.

"This rather makeshift plan I proceeded to execute. Transporting the material to the middle of the weed-grown space, I covered it lightly with twigs and various articles of loose rubbish. It was now quite invisible, and I was turning away to go when suddenly I bethought me of the dry preparation of the head that ought to accompany the skeleton. Without that, the specimen would be incomplete; and an incomplete specimen would spoil the series. I reflected awhile. It seemed a pity to spoil the completeness of the series for the sake of a little trouble. I had a good-sized bag with me and a quantity of stout brown paper in it in which the bulbs had been wrapped. Why not?

"In the end, I decided that the series should not be spoilt. I need not describe the obvious details of the simple procedure. When I came up out of the chalk-pit a quarter of an hour later, my bag contained the material for the required preparation of a mummified head.

"I soon struck the familiar footpath and set forth at a brisk pace to catch the late train from Gravesend. It was a long walk and a pleasant one, though the bag was uncomfortably heavy. I thought, with grim amusement, of Grayson's gang of footpads. It would be a quaint situation if I encountered some of them and was robbed of my bag. The possibilities that the idea opened out were highly diverting and kept me entertained until I at last reached Gravesend Station and was bundled by the guard into a first-class compartment just as the train was starting. I should have preferred an empty compartment, but there was no choice; and as three of the corners were occupied, I took possession of the fourth. The rack over my seat was occupied by a bag about the size of my own, apparently the property of a clergyman who sat in the opposite corner, so I had to place my bag in the rack over his head.

"I watched him during the journey as he sat opposite me reading the Church Times and wondered how he would feel if he knew what was in the bag above him. Probably he would have been quite disturbed; for many of these clerics entertain the quaintest of old-world ideas. And he was mighty near to knowing, too; for when the train had stopped at Hither Green and was just about to move off, he suddenly sprang up, exclaiming, 'God bless my soul!' and snatching my bag from the rack, darted out on the platform. I immediately grabbed his bag from my rack and rushed out after him as the train started, hailing him to stop. 'Hi! My good sir! You've taken my bag.'

"'Not at all,' he replied indignantly. 'You're quite mistaken.' And then, as I held out his own bag, he looked from one to the other, and, to my horror, pressed the clasp of my bag and pulled it wide open.

"On what small chances do great events turn! But for the brown paper in my bag, there would have been a catastrophe. As it was, when his eye lighted on that rough, globular paper parcel he handed me my bag with an apologetic smirk and received his own in exchange. But after that, I kept my property in my hand until I was safe within the precincts of my laboratory.

"The usual disappointment awaited me when I came to examine the hair and finger-prints. He was not the man whom I sought. But he made an acceptable addition to the Series of Criminal Anthropology in my museum, for I duly collected the bones from the great nettle-bed in the chalk-pit early in the following September, and set them, properly bleached and riveted together, in the large wall-case. But this specimen had a further, though indirect, value. From him I gathered a useful hint by which I was subsequently guided into a new and fruitful field of research. "(See Catalogue, Numbers 6A and 6B.)"

V

BY-PRODUCTS OF INDUSTRY

The next entry in the amazing "Museum Archives" exhibited my poor friend Humphrey Challoner in circumstances that were to me perfectly incredible. When I recall that learned, cultivated man as I knew him, I find it impossible to picture him living amidst the indescribably squalid surroundings of the London Ghetto, the tenant of a sordid little shop in an East End by-street. Yet this appears actually to have been his condition at one time—but let me quote the entry in his own words, which need no comments of mine to heighten their strangeness.

"Events connected with the acquirement of Numbers 7, 8 and 9 in the Anthropological Series:

"We are the creatures of circumstance. Blind chance, which guided that unknown wretch to my house in the dead of the night and which led my dear wife to her death at his murderous hands, also impelled that other villain (Number 6, Anthropological Series) to pursue me to the lonely chalk-pit, where he would have done me to death had I not fortunately anticipated his intentions. So, too, it was by a mere chance that I presently found myself the proprietor of a shop in a Whitechapel back-street.

"Let me trace the connections of events.

"The first link in the chain was a visit that I had paid in my younger days to Moscow and Warsaw, where I had stayed long enough to acquire a useful knowledge of Russian and Yiddish. The second link was the failure of my plan to lure the murderer of my wife—and, incidentally, other criminals—to my house. The trap had been scented not only by the criminals but also by the police, of whom one had visited my museum with very evident suspicion as to the nature of my specimens.

"After the visit of the detective, I was rather at a loose end. That unknown wretch was still at large. He had to be found and I had to find him since the police could not. But how? That detective

73

had completely upset my plans and, for a time, I could think of no other. Then came the dirty rascal who had tried to murder me in the chalk-pit; and from his mongrel jargon, half cockney, half foreign, I had gathered a vague hint. If I could not entice the criminal population into my domain, how would it be to reconnoiter theirs? The alien area of London was well known to me, for it had always seemed interesting since my visit to Warsaw, and, judging from the police reports, it appeared to be a veritable happy hunting-ground for the connoisseur in criminals.

"Hence it was that my unrest led me almost daily to perambulate that strange region east of Aldgate where uncouth foreign names stare out from the shop signs and almost every public or private notice is in the Hebrew character. Dressed in my shabbiest clothes, I trudged, hour after hour and day after day, through the gray and joyless streets and alleys, looking earnestly into the beady eyes and broad faces of the East-European wayfarers and wondering whether any of them was the man I sought.

"One evening, as I was returning homeward through the district that lies at the rear of Middlesex Street, my attention was arrested by a large card tacked on the door of a closed shop. A dingy barber's pole gave a clue to the nature of the industry formerly carried on, and the card—which was written upon in fair and even scholarly Hebrew characters—supplied particulars. I had stopped to read the inscription, faintly amused at the incongruity between the recondite Oriental lettering and the matter-of-fact references to 'eligible premises' and 'fixtures and goodwill,' when the door opened and two men came out. One was a typical English Jew, smart, chubby and prosperous; the other was evidently a foreigner.

"Both men stood aside to enable me to continue my reading, and, as I was about to turn away, the smarter of the two addressed me.

"'Good chanth here, misther. Nithe little bithness going for nothing. No charge for goodwill or fixtures. Ready-made bithneth and nothing to pay but rent.'

"'Ja!' the other man broke in, 'dat shop is a leedle goldmine; und you buys 'im for noding.'

"It was an absurd situation. I was beginning smilingly to shake my head when the Jew resumed eagerly:

"I tell you, misther, itth a chanth in a million. A firth clath bithneth and not a brown to pay for the goodwill. Come in and have a look round,' he added persuasively.

"I suppose I am curious by nature. At any rate, I am sure it was nothing but idle curiosity to see what the interior of a Whitechapel house was like that led me to follow the two men into the dark and musty-smelling shop. But hardly had my eyes lighted on the frowsy fixtures and appurtenances of the trade when there flashed into my mind a really luminous idea.

"'Why did the last man leave?' I asked.

"The Jew caught the lapel of my coat and exclaimed impressively:

"'The lath man wath a fool. Got himself mixthed up with the crookth. Thet up a roulette table in the thellar and let 'em come and gamble away their thwag. Thtoopid thing to do, though, mind you, he did a rare good line while it lathted. Got the sthuff for nothing, you thee.' His tone at this point was regretfully sympathetic.

"'What happened in the end?' I asked.

"'The copperth dropped on him. Thomebody gave him away.'

"'Some of the ladies, perhaps,' I suggested.

"'Ach! Zo!' the other man burst in fiercely, 'Of gourse it vas der vimmen! It is always der vimmen. Dese dam vimmen, dey makes all der drabble!' He thumped the table with his fist, and then, catching the Hebrew's eye, suddenly subsided into silence.

"From the shop we proceeded to the little parlor behind, from which a door gave access, by a flight of most dangerous stone steps, to the large cellar. This was lighted by a grating from the back yard, with which it also communicated by a flight of steps and a door. We next examined the yard itself, a small paved enclosure with a gate opening on an alley, and occupied at the moment by an empty beer-barrel, a builder's hand-cart and a dead cat.

"'Like to thee the upstairth roomth?' inquired the Hebrew gentleman, whose name I understood to be Nathan. I nodded abstractedly and followed him up the stairs, gathering a general

75

impression of all-pervading dirt. The upper rooms were of no interest to me after what I had seen downstairs.

"'Well,' said Mr. Nathan when we were once more back in the shop, 'what do you think of it?'

"I did not answer his question literally. If I had, I should have startled him. For I thought the place absolutely ideal for my purpose. Just consider its potentialities! I was searching for a criminal whom I could identify by his hair. Here was a barber's shop in the heart of a criminal neighborhood and admittedly the late haunt of criminals. Those criminals were certain to come back. I could examine their hair at my leisure; and—there was the cellar. It was, I repeat, absolutely ideal.

"'I think the place will suit me,' I said.

"Mr. Nathan beamed on me. 'Of courth,' he said, 'referentheth will be nethethary, or rent in advanthe.'

"'A year's rent in advance will do, I suppose?' said I; and Mr. Nathan nearly jumped clear off the floor. A few minutes later I departed, the accepted tenant (under the pseudonym of Simon Vosper) of Samuel Nathan, with the understanding that I should deliver my advance rent in bank-notes and that he should have the top-dressing of dirt removed from the house and the name of Vosper painted over the shop.

"My preparations for the new activities on which I was to enter were quickly made. In my Bloomsbury house I installed as caretaker a retired sergeant-major of incomparable taciturnity. I locked up the museum wing and kept the keys. I took a few lessons in haircutting from a West-End barber. I paid my advance rent, sent in a set of bedroom furniture to my new premises in Saul Street, Whitechapel, abandoned the habit of shaving for some ten days, and then took possession of the shop.

"At first the customers were few and far between. A stray coster or carman came in from time to time, but mostly the shop was silent and desolate. But this did not distress me. I had various preparations to make and a plan of campaign to settle. There were the cellar stairs, for instance; a steep flight of stone steps, unguarded by baluster or handrail. They were very dangerous. But when I had fitted a sort of giant stride by suspending a stout rope from the ceiling, I was able to swing myself down the whole flight in perfect safety. Other preparations consisted in the placing, of an iron safe in the parlor (with a small mirror above it) and the purchase of a tin of stiff cart-grease and a few large barrels. These latter I bought from a cooper in the form of staves and hoops, and built them up in the cellar in my rather extensive spare time.

"Meanwhile trade gradually increased. The harmless coster and laborer began to be varied by customers rather more in my line; in fact, I had not quite completed my arrangements when I got the first windfall.

"It was a Wednesday evening. I had nearly finished shaving a large, military-looking laborer when the door opened very quietly and a seedy, middle-aged man entered and sat down. His movements were silent—almost stealthy; and, when he had seated himself, he picked up a newspaper from behind which I saw him steal furtive and suspicious glances at the patient in the operating chair. The latter, being scraped clean, rose to depart, and the newcomer underwent a total eclipse behind the newspaper.

"'Oo's 'e?' he demanded, when the laborer was safely outside.

"'I don't know him,' I replied, 'but I should say, by his hands, a laborer.'

"'Looked rather like a copper,' said my customer. He took his place in the vacated chair with a laconic "Air cut,' and then became conversational.

"'So you've took on Polensky's job?'

"I nodded at the mirror that faced us (Polensky was my predecessor) and he continued, 'Polensky's doing time, ain't he?'

"I believed he was and said so, and my friend then asked:

"'Young Pongo ever come in here now?'

"Naturally I had never heard of young Pongo, but I felt that I must not appear too ignorant. It were better to invent a little.

"'Pongo,' I ruminated; 'Pongo. Is that the fellow who was with Joe Bartels in that job at—er—you know?'

"'No, I don't,' said my friend. 'And 'oo's Joe Bartels?'

"'Oh, I thought you knew him; but if you don't I'd better say no more. You see, I don't know who you are.'

"'Don't yer. Then I'll tell yer. I'm Spotty Bamber, of Spitalfields, that's 'oo I am. So now you know.'

"I made a mental note of the name (the first part of which had apparently been suggested by Mr. Bamber's complexion) and my attention must have wandered somewhat, for my patient suddenly shouted: 'Ere! I say! I didn't come 'ere to be scalped. I come to 'ave my 'air cut.'

"I apologized and led the conversation back to Polensky.

"'Ah,' said Bamber, "e was a downy un, 'e was. Bit too downy. Opened his mouth too wide. Wanted it all for nix. That was why he got peached on—' Here Spotty turned his head with a jerk—'What are you looking at me through that thing for? My 'ed ain't as small as all that.'

"'That thing' was a Coddington lens, through which I examined the hair of every customer with a view to identification. But I did not tell Mr. Bamber this. My explanation was recondite and rather obscure, but it seemed to satisfy him.

"'Well,' he said, 'you're a rum cove. Talk like a blooming toff too, you do.' I made a careful mental note of that fact and determined to study the local dialect. Meanwhile I explained, 'I wasn't always a hairdresser, you know.'

"'So I should suppose,' answered Spotty, twisting his neck to get a look at his poll in the glass. 'What you'd call a bloomin' ammerchewer.' He stood up, shook himself and tendered a half-crown in payment, which I examined carefully before giving change. Then I brought out of my pocket a handful of assorted coins, including two sovereigns, a quantity of silver and some coppers. I do not ordinarily carry my money mixed up in this slovenly fashion, but had adopted the habit, since I came to the shop, for a definite reason; and was now justified by the avaricious glare that lighted up in Spotty's eye at the sight of the coins in my hand.

"I picked out his change deliberately and handed it to him, when he took it and stood for a few seconds, evidently thinking hard. Suddenly he thrust his hand into his pocket and said, 'I suppose, mister, you haven't got such a thing as a fi-pun-note what

78

you can give me in exchange for five jimmies?' He held out five sovereigns, which I took from him and inspected critically.

"'Oh, they're all right,' said Spotty, as I weighed them in my hand. And so they were.

"'I think I can let you have a note if you will wait a moment,' I said; and, as I turned to enter the parlor, Spotty sat down ostentatiously in the chair.

"I drew the door to after me, but did not latch it. A small jet of gas was burning in the parlor and by its light I unlocked the safe, pulled out a drawer, took from it a bundle of banknotes and looked them over; all very deliberately and with my eye on the mirror that hung above the safe. That mirror reflected the door. It also reflected me, but as the light was on my back my face was in the shadow. Hardly had I opened the safe when, slowly and silently, the door opened a couple of inches and an eye appeared in the space. I picked a note out of the bundle, returned the remainder to the drawer, closed the safe and slowly walked to the door. When I re-entered the shop, Spotty was seated in the chair as I had left him, with the immovable air of an Egyptian statue.

"I have no doubt that Spotty Bamber chuckled with joy when he got outside. I should like to think so, to feel that our pleasure was mutual. For as to me, my feelings can only be appreciated by some patient angler who, after a long and fruitless sitting, has seen his

"'quill or cork down sink
With eager bite of perch or bleak or dace.'

"Spotty was on the hook. He would come again, and not alone—at least, I trusted not alone. For my brief inspection of his hair had convinced me that he was not the unknown man whom I sought; and, though he would make an acceptable addition to the group of specimens in the long wall-case, I was more interested in the companion whom I felt confident he would bring with him. The elation of spirit produced by the prospect of this second visit was such that I forthwith closed the shop and spent the rest of the evening exercising with the concussor and practicing flying leaps down the cellar steps with the aid of the giant-stride.

"I slept little that night. As a special precaution against failure, I had left the back gate unbolted and refrained from locking the outside cellar door; with the sole result that I was roused up at one in the morning by a meddlesome constable and rebuked sourly for my carelessness. Otherwise, not a soul came to enliven my solitude. The second night passed in the same dull fashion, leaving me restless and disappointed; and when the third slipped by without the sign of a visitor, I became really uneasy.

"The fourth day was Saturday, and the late evening—the end of the Sabbath—turned my shop into a veritable Land of Goshen. The conversation, mostly in Yiddish—of which I professed total ignorance—kept me pretty well amused until closing time arrived. Then, as the shop emptied, my hopes and fears began to revive together.

"I was about to begin shutting up the premises when the door opened softly and a man slipped into the shop. My heart leaped exultingly. The man was Spotty Bamber.

"And he was not alone. By no means. Two more men stole in in the same stealthy fashion, and, having first glanced at one another and then peered suspiciously round the shop, they all looked at me. For my part, I regarded them with deep interest, especially as to their hair. 'Habitual Criminal' was written large on all of them. As anthropological material they were quite excellent.

"Mr. Bamber opened the proceedings with one eye on me and the other on the door.

"'Look, 'ere, mister, we've come about a little matter of business. You know Polensky used to do a bit of trade?'

"'Yes,' I said; 'and now he's doing a bit of time.'

"'I know,' replied Spotty, 'but you must take the fat with the lean. It ain't all soup. And you know that Polensky was a bloomin' fool.'

"'It comes to this 'ere,' said one of the other men, stepping up close to me. 'Do you know a jerry when you sees one—a red 'un, mind you?'

"As I had not the faintest idea what the man meant, I temporized.

"'I haven't seen one yet, you know.'

"The fellow looked furtively at the door and then, diving into an inner pocket, pulled out a handsome gold watch with a massive chain attached, exhibited it for a moment and then dropped it back.

"'That's the little article,' said he, 'and before you makes a bid, you can look it over and try if the stuff's genu-wine. But not out here, you know. We does our deal inside where you can't get ogled by a copper through the winder.'

"I saw the plan at a glance, and, in the main, approved, though three at once was a bigger handful than I should have desired. They would require careful treatment.

"'I will just go and see that it's all clear,' I said; and with this I retired to the parlor, quietly bolting the door behind me.

"Once inside, I made my simple preparations rapidly. Placing the concussor in a tall cylindrical basket close to the cellar door, I opened the latter and hitched the rope in a position where I could grasp it easily. Then I took from the cupboard the tin of cart-grease, and, with a large knife, spread a thick layer of the grease on the upper four steps of the cellar stairs. While thus engaged, I turned over my plans quickly but with considerable misgivings. The odds were greater than I ought to have taken. For, as to the intentions of these men, I could have no reasonable doubt. Bamber was known to me and he would not run the risk of my giving information. The amiable intention of these gentry was to 'do me in,' as they would have expressed it, and the vital question for me was, How did they mean to do it? Firearms they would probably avoid on account of the noise, but if they all came at me at once with knives my chance would be infinitesimal.

"It comes back to me now rather oddly that I weighed these probabilities quite impersonally, as though I were a mere spectator. And such was virtually the case. The fact is that, although I had long since abandoned the idea of suicide, I remained alive as a matter of principle and not by personal desire. My objection to being killed was merely the abstract objection to the killing of any worthy member of society by these human vermin. But if any such

81

person must needs be killed, I was quite indifferent as to whether the subject of the action were myself or some other. I had no personal interest in the matter. Hence, when I unbolted the door and beckoned the three men into the room, though doubtful of the issue, I had no feeling of nervousness.

"The advantage that my impassiveness gave me over those three rascals was very evident when they slouched in, for they were all trembling and twitching with nervous excitement. And no wonder. To a man who values his life above everything on earth, it is a serious matter to walk into the very shadow of the gallows. As soon as they were inside, one of them, who looked like a Polish Jew, bolted the door; and then they gathered round me like a pack of hyenas.

"I backed unostentatiously into the corner by the cellar door, talking volubly to the three men by turn as I went; and the Jew edged along the wall to get behind me. I realized that he was the one whom I had to watch, and I watched him; not looking at him, but keeping him on the periphery of my field of vision. For, as is well known, the peripheral area of the retina, although insensitive to impressions of form, is highly sensitive to impressions of movement.

"My remarks on the danger to respectable persons of meddling with stolen property gave Mr. Bamber his cue.

"'Stolen property,' he roared. "Oo said anything about stolen property? What d'yer mean, yer bloomin' scalp-scraper!' and he advanced threateningly with his chin stuck forward and a most formidable scowl.

"In the next few moments I reaped the reward of my strenuous practice at the gymnasium of the art of Jiu-jitsu and the French style of boxing. Bamber's advance was the signal. I had seen the Jew's hand steal under his coat skirt. He now made a quick movement—and so did I. Whisking round, in an instant I had his wrist in that kind of grip that dislocates the elbow-joint, and, as I turned, I planted my foot heavily on Spotty Bamber's chest. The swift movement took them all by surprise. The Jew screamed and dropped his knife, staggering heavily against the cellar door, which swung back on its well-oiled hinges. Bamber flew backwards like a football, and, as he cannoned against the third man, the two crashed together to the floor. I thrust the Jew through the open doorway, released his wrist; and then followed a slithering sound from the cellar steps, ending in a soft thump.

"The position was marvelously changed in those few moments. The Jew, I took it, was eliminated, and the odds thus brought down to a reasonable figure. As to the other two, though they scrambled to their feet quickly enough, they kept their distance, Bamber in particular having some little difficulty with his breath. I picked up the concussor and faced them. If I had been quick, I could have dispatched them both without difficulty. But I did not. Once more I was aware of that singular state of consciousness to which I have elsewhere alluded as possessing me in the presence of violent criminals; a vivid pleasure in the mere act of physical contest, perfectly incomprehensible to me in my normal state of mind. This strange joy now sent the blood surging through my brain until my ears hummed; and yet I kept my judgment, calmly attentive and even wary.

"Thus, when the third ruffian rushed at me with a large sheath-knife, I knocked his hand aside quite neatly with the concussor and drove him out of range with a heavy blow of my left fist. But at this moment I observed Bamber frantically lugging something from his hip-pocket; something that was certainly not a knife. It was time for a change of tactics. Before the third rascal could close with me again, I darted at the open doorway, grasped the rope, and in an instant had swung myself clear of the steps down into the darkness of the cellar.

"In swinging I had turned half round, and, as I alighted, I saw my aggressor, knife in hand, come through the doorway in pursuit. He had more courage than Spotty but less discretion. In the haste of his pursuit, he actually sprang over the sill on to the slippery top step, and the next moment was bumping down the stairs like an overturned sack of potatoes. As he picked himself up, half-stunned, from the prostrate Jew, on whom he had fallen, I regretfully felled him with the concussor. It was a dull finish to the affair, but there was Bamber's revolver to be reckoned with.

"To do Mr. Bamber justice, he was not rash. In fact, he was so unobtrusive that I began to fear that he had made off, and, it being obviously unsafe to go up and ascertain, I proceeded to make a few encouraging demonstrations.

"'Oh!' I shouted, 'Let me go! Let go my hands or I'll call for the police!'

"This appeal had the desired effect. The dimly lighted doorway framed the figure of Spotty Bamber, with revolver poised, peering cautiously into the darkness.

"I renewed my protests, and, retiring to the darkest corner, shuffled noisily about the brick floor.

"''Ave yer got 'im, Alf?' inquired the discreet Bamber, leaning forward and stepping over the sill. I continued to dance heavily in my corner and to utter breathless snorts and exclamations such as, 'Let go, I tell you!' 'Aha! would you?' and so forth. Bamber took another step forward, craned his neck and called out, 'Shove 'im over this way, Alf, so as I can—'

"He did not finish the sentence. Watching him, I saw his feet suddenly fly from under him, the revolver clattered on the cellar floor, and Spotty, himself, having slipped half-way down the steps, fell over the edge on to the hard brick pavement.

"As he picked himself up, breathing heavily, I dropped the concussor into the big pocket of my apron and pounced on him. He uttered a yell of terror and began to struggle like a maniac to free himself from my grip, while I edged him away from the dangerous vicinity of the revolver. At first he was disposed to show a good deal of fight, and, as we gyrated round the cellar, tugging, thrusting, wrenching and kicking, I found the strenuous muscular exercise strangely exhilarating. Evidently there is something to be said for the 'simple life,' as lived in those primitive communities where every man is his own policeman.

"But this physically stimulating bout came to a sudden end. Our mazy revolutions brought us presently near the foot of the steps, and here Spotty tripped over the prostrate form of the third man. He staggered back a few paces and uttered a husky shriek, and then we came down together on top of the Jew. That finished him. The contact with those two motionless shapes shattered his

84

nerves utterly and reduced him to sheer panic. He ceased to fight and only whimpered for mercy.

"It was very unpleasant. As long as the fight was hot and strenuous, the revived instincts of long-forgotten primitive ancestors kept my blood racing. But, with the first cry for mercy, all my exhilaration died out and the degenerate emotions of civilized man began to make themselves felt. If I hesitated I was lost. At every pitiful bleat I felt myself weakening. There was only one thing to do, and I did it—with the concussor.

"Verbal description is a slow affair compared with action. The whole set of events that I have narrated occupied but a few minutes. When I unbolted the parlor door and found a somnolent navvy waiting to be shaved, I realized with astonishment how brief the interlude had been.

"'Hope I haven't kept you waiting,' I said, anxious to learn if he had heard anything unusual.

"'No,' he replied, 'I've only just come in. Didn't expect to find you open.'

"He seated himself in the chair and I lathered him profusely, with luxurious pleasure in handling the clean soapsuds. The folly of my late visitors in leaving the shop door unfastened, surprised me, and illustrated afresh the poverty of the criminal intelligence. They had assumed that it would be all over in a moment and had taken no precautions against the improbable. And such is the 'habitual' with whom the costly machinery of the law is unable to cope! Verily, there must be a good many fools besides the dishonest ones!

"I shut up the shop when my customer departed, indulged in a good wash and a substantial supper. For there was much to be done before I could go to bed. I had providently laid in six casks of a suitable size, of which two were put together and the remainder in the form of loose staves and hoops. One of these would have to be made up at once, since it was necessary that the specimens should be packed before rigor mortis set in and rendered them unmanageable. Accordingly, I fell to work after supper with the mallet and the broad chisel-like tool with which the hoops are driven on, and did not pause until the bundle of staves was converted into a cask, complete save for the top hoop and head.

"I proceeded systematically. Into one cask I poured a quart of water and wetted the interior thoroughly, to make the wood swell and secure tight joints. Then into it I introduced the Jew, in a sitting posture, and was gratified to find that the specimen occupied the space comfortably. But here a slight difficulty presented itself. The center of gravity of a cask filled with homogeneous matter coincides with the geometrical center. But in a cask containing a deceased Jew, the center of gravity would be markedly ex-centric. Such a cask would not roll evenly; and irregular rolling might lead to investigation. However, the remedy was quite simple. My predecessor had been accustomed to cover the floor of the shop with sawdust, and the peculiar habits of my customers had led me to continue the practice. An immense bin of the material occupied a corner of the cellar and furnished the means of imparting a factitious homogeneity to the contents of the cask. I shoveled in a quantity around the specimen, headed up the cask, and finished filling it through the bung-hole. When I had driven in the bung, I gave the cask a trial roll on the cellar floor and found that it moved without noticeable irregularity.

"It was past midnight before I had finished my labors and had the three casks ready for removal. After another good wash, I went to bed, and, thanks to the invigorating physical exercise, had an excellent night.

"The following day being Sunday, there was a regrettable delay, since it would have been unwise to challenge attention by trundling the casks through the streets when all the world was resting. However, I called at my Bloomsbury house and instructed the sergeant-major that some packages might be delivered on the following day. 'And,' I added, 'I shall probably be working in the laboratory tomorrow, so if you hear me moving about you will know that it is all right.'

"The sergeant-major touched his cap—he always wore a cap indoors—without speaking. He was the most taciturn and incurious man that I have ever met.

"When I had taken a look round the laboratory and made a few preparations, I departed, going out by the museum entrance. It was as well to get the sergeant-major used to these casual, unannounced appearances and disappearances. I walked slowly back to Whitechapel, turning over my plans for the removal of the casks. At first I had thought of taking them to Pickford's receiving office. But there was danger in this, though it was a remote danger. If one of the casks should be accidentally dropped it would certainly burst, and then—I had no particular objection to being killed, but I had a very great objection to being sent to Broadmoor. So I decided to effect the removal myself with the aid of the builder's truck that I had allowed the owner to keep in my yard. But this plan involved the adoption of some sort of disguise; a very slight one would be sufficient, as it was merely to prevent recognition by casual strangers.

"Now, among the stock of my predecessor, Polensky, I had found a collection of powder colors, grease paints, toupée-paste, spirit-gum and other materials which threw a curious light on his activities. On my return to the shop I made a few experiments with these materials and was astonished to find on what trivial peculiarities facial expression depends. For instance, I discovered that a strip of court-plaster, carried tightly up the middle of the forehead—where it would be hidden by a hat—altered the angle of the eyebrows and completely changed the expression, and that a thin scumble of purple, rubbed on the nose, totally altered the character of the face. This was deeply interesting; and, as it finally disposed of one difficulty, it left me free to consider the rest of my plans, which I continued to do until every possible emergency was anticipated and provided for.

"Early on Monday morning I went out and purchased four lengths of stout quartering—two long and two short—a coil of rope, a two-block tackle of the kind known to mariners as a 'handy Billy' and a pair of cask-grips. With the quartering and some lengths of rope I made two cask-slides, a long one for the cellar and a short one for the hand-cart. Placing the long slide in position, I greased it with cart-grease, hooked the tackle above the upper end, attached the grips and very soon had the three casks hoisted up into the passage that opened into the back yard. With the aid of the short slide and the tackle, I ran them up into the cart, lashed them firmly in position with the stout rope, threw in the slide and tackle and was ready to start. Running into the shop, I fixed the necessary strip of court-plaster on my forehead, tinted my nose, and, having pocketed the stick of paint and a piece of plaster, put on my shabbiest overcoat and a neck-cloth, trod on my hat and jammed it on my head so that it should cover the strip of plaster. Then I went out and, trundling the cart into the alley, locked the back gate and set forth on my journey.

"Navigating the crowded streets with the heavy cart clattering behind me, I made my way westward, avoiding the main thoroughfares with their bewildering traffic, until I found myself in Theobald's Row at the end of Red Lion Street. Here I began to look about for a likely deputy; and presently my eye lighted on a sturdy-looking man who leaned somewhat dejectedly against a post and sucked at an empty pipe. He was evidently not a regular 'corner-boy.' I judged him to be a laborer out of work, and deciding that he would serve my purpose I addressed him.

"'Want a job, mate?'

"He roused at once. 'You've 'it it, mate. I do. What sort of job?'

"'Pull this truck round to 6A Plimsbury Street and deliver the tubs.'

"'Ow much 'll you give me?' was the inevitable inquiry.

"'Old chap'll give you half-a-crown, if you ask him.'

"'And 'ow much am I to keep?'

"'Oh, we won't quarrel about that. I've got to see about another job or I'd take 'em myself. You deliver the tubs—and be careful of 'em. They're full of valuable chemicals—and meet me here at ten o'clock and I'll give you another job. Will that do you?'

"My friend pocketed his pipe and spat on his hands. 'Gi' me the bloomin' truck,' said he; and when I had surrendered the pole to him, he set off at a pace that made me thankful for the stout rope lashings of the casks.

"I let him draw ahead and then followed at a discreet distance, keeping him in sight until he was within a few hundred yards of my house. Then I darted down a side turning, took a short cut across a square, and, arriving at the museum entrance, let myself in with my Yale key.

"To remove my hat, overcoat and coat, to tear off the plaster and wash my nose, was but the work of a minute. I had placed in readiness my laboratory apron, a velvet skull-cap and a pair of spectacles, and scarcely had I assumed these and settled my eyebrows into a studious frown, when the bell rang. A glance into a little mirror that hung on the wall satisfied me as to the radical change in my appearance and I went out confidently and opened the street door. My deputy was standing on the door-step and touched his cap nervously as he met my portentous frown.

"'These here barrils for you, sir?' he asked.

"'Quite right,' I replied in deep, pompous tones; 'I will help you to bring them in.'

"We brought the cart up on the pavement with the pole across the threshold, and I fixed the slide in position while my assistant cast off the lashings. In a couple of minutes we had run the casks down the slide and I had the satisfaction of seeing them safely deposited in the hall. The dangers and difficulties of the passage were at an end.

"I handed my proxy the half-crown which he sheepishly demanded, with an extra shilling 'for a glass of beer,' and saw him go on his way rejoicing. Then I went back to the laboratory, stuck on a fresh strip of plaster, rubbed on a tint of grease-paint and resumed my disreputable garments. When I came forth into the street, the hand-cart had already disappeared, leaving me to pursue my way unobserved to the rendezvous, where I presently met my friend, and, having rejoiced him with a further shilling, resumed possession of the cart.

"On my arrival at my Whitechapel premises, I affixed a notice to the window informing the nobility and gentry that I was 'absent on business.' Then I clothed myself decently, emptied the contents of the safe into a hand-bag, in which I also put the cooper's chisel, locked up the premises and hurried off to Aldgate Station. My first objective was the establishment of Mr. Hammerstein, the dealer in osteology, from whom I purchased three articulated human skeletons, and obtained the invaluable receipted invoices; and having thus taken every precaution that prudence and human foresight could suggest, I repaired to my Bloomsbury house, let myself in at the museum door, rolled the casks through into the laboratory and proceeded to unpack the specimens.

"The initial processes occupied me far into the night, while as to the finishing operations, they kept me busy for over a month; during which time I shaved and cut hair throughout the day up to nine o'clock at night, reserving the laboratory work for a relaxation after the prosaic labors of the day.

"Looked at broadly, the episode was highly satisfactory and successful—excepting in one vital respect. None of the three specimens had ringed hair. The completed preparations were, after all, but the by-products of my industry. The wretch whom I sought was still at large and unidentified. My collection still lacked its crowning ornament."

VI

THE TRAIL OF THE SERPENT

Hitherto, in my transcriptions from Humphrey Challoner's "Museum Archives" I have taken the entries in their order, omitting only such technical details as might seem unsuitable for the lay reader. Now, however, I pass over a number of entries. The capture of Numbers 7, 8 and 9 exhibits the methods to which Challoner, in the main, adhered during his long residence in East London; and, though there were occasional variations, the accounts of the captures present a general similarity which might render their recital tedious. The last entry but one, on the other hand, is among the most curious and interesting. Apart from the stirring incidents that it records, the new light that it throws on a hitherto unsolved mystery makes it worth extracting entire, which I now proceed to do, with the necessary omissions alluded to above.

"Circumstances connected with the acquirement of Numbers 23 and 24 in the Anthropological Series.

"The sand of my life ran out with varying speed—as it seemed to me—in the little barber's shop in Saul Street, Whitechapel. Now would my pulses beat and the current of my blood run swift. Those were the times when I had visitors; and presently a new skeleton or two would make their appearance in the long wall-case. But there were long intervals of sordid labor and dull inaction when I would cut hair—and examine it through my lens—day after day and wonder whether, in electing to live, rather than pass voluntarily into eternal repose, I had, after all, chosen the better part. For in all those years no customer with ringed hair ever came to my shop. The long pursuit seemed to bring me no nearer to that unknown wretch, the slayer of my beloved wife. Still was he hidden from me amidst the unclean multitude that seethed around; or perchance some sordid grave had already offered him an everlasting sanctuary, leaving me wearily to pursue a phantom enemy.

"But I am digressing. This is not a record of my emotions, but a history of the contents of my museum. Let me proceed to specimens 23 and 24 and the very remarkable circumstances under which I had the good fortune to acquire them. First, however, I must describe an incident which, although it occurred some time before, never developed its importance until this occasion arose.

"One drowsy afternoon there came to my shop a smallish, shabby-looking man, quiet and civil in manner and peculiarly wooden as to his countenance; in short, a typical 'old lag.' I recognized the type at a glance; the 'penal servitude face' had become a familiar phenomenon. He spread himself out to be shaved and to have the severely official style of his coiffure replaced by a less distinctive mode; and as I worked he conversed affably.

"'Saw old Polensky a week or two ago.'

"'Did you indeed?' said I.

"'Yus. Portland. Got into 'ot water, too, 'e did. Tried to fetch the farm and didn't pull it orf.' ('The farm,' I may explain, is the prison infirmary.) 'Got dropped on for malingering. That's the way with these bloomin' foreigners.'

"'He didn't impose on the doctor, then?'

"'Lor', no! Doctor'd seen that sort o' bloke before. Polensky said he'd got a pain in 'is stummik, so the doctor says it must be becos 'is diet was too rich, and knocks orf arf 'is grub. I tell yer, Polensky was sorry 'e'd spoke.'

"Here, my client showing a disposition to smile, I removed the razor to allow him to do so. Presently he resumed, discursively:

"'I knoo this 'ouse years ago, before Polensky's time, when old Durdler had it. Durdler used to do the smashin' lay up on the second floor and me and two or three nippers used to work for 'im—plantin' the snide, yer know. 'E was a rare leery un, was Durdler. It was 'im what made that slidin' door in the wall in the second floor front.'

"I pricked up my ears at this. 'A sliding door? In this house?'

"'Gawblimy!' exclaimed my client. 'Meantersay you don't know about that door?'

"I assured him most positively that I had never heard of it.

92

"'Well, well,' he muttered. 'Sich a useful thing, too. Durdler used to keep 'is molds and stuff up there, and then, when there was a scare of the cops, he used to pop the thing through into the next 'ouse — Mrs. Jacob 'ad the room next door — and the coppers used to come and sniff round, but of course there wasn't nothin' to see. Regler suck in for them. And it was useful if you was follered. You could mizzle in through the shop, run upstairs, pop through the door, downstairs next door and out through the back yard. I've done it myself. 'Oo's got the second floor front now?'

"'I have,' said I. 'I keep the whole of the house.'

"'My eye!' exclaimed my friend, whose name I learned to be Towler, 'you are a bloomin' toff. Like me to show you that door?'

"I said that I should like it very much, and accordingly, when the trimming operations were concluded and I had secured a wisp of Mr. Towler's hair for subsequent examination, we ascended to the second floor front and he demonstrated the hidden door.

"'It's in this 'ere cupboard, under that row of pegs. That peg underneath at the side is the 'andle. You catches 'old of it, so, and you gives a pull to the right.' He suited the action to the words, and, with a loud groan, the middle third of the back of the cupboard slid bodily to the right, leaving an opening about three feet square, beyond which was a solid-looking panel with a small knob at the left-hand side.

"'That,' whispered Towler, 'is the back of a cupboard in the next 'ouse. If you was to pull that 'andle to the right, it would slide along same as this one. Only I expect there's somebody in the room there.'

"I rewarded Mr. Towler with half a sovereign, which he evidently thought liberal, and he departed gleefully. Shortly afterwards I learned that he had 'got a stretch' in connection with a 'job' at Camberwell; and he vanished from my ken. But I did not forget the sliding doors. No special use for them suggested itself, but their potentialities were so obvious that I resolved to keep a sharp eye on the second floor front next door.

"I had not long to wait. Presently the whole floor was advertised by a card on the street door as being to let and I seized the opportunity of a quiet Sunday to reconnoiter and put the arrangements in going order. I slid back the panel on my own side and then, dragging at the handle, pushed back the second panel. Both moved noisily and would require careful treatment. I passed through the square opening into the vacant room and looked round, but there was little to see, though a good deal to smell, for the windows were hermetically sealed and a closed stove fitted into the fireplace precluded any possibility of ventilation. The aroma of the late tenants still lingered in the air.

"I returned through the opening and began my labors. First, with a hard brush I cleaned out both sets of grooves, top and bottom. Then, into each groove I painted a thick coating of tallow and black lead, mixed into a paste and heated. By moving the panels backwards and forwards a great number of times I distributed the lubricant and brought the black lead to such a polish that the doors slid with the greatest ease and without a sound. I was so pleased with the result that I was tempted to engage the room next door, but as this might have aroused suspicion—seeing that I had a whole house already—I refrained; and shortly afterwards the floor was taken by a family of Polish Jews, who apparently supplemented their income by letting part of it furnished.

"I now pass over an intervening period and come to the circumstances of one of my most interesting and stirring experiences. It was about this time that some misbegotten mechanician invented the automatic magazine pistol, and thereby rendered possible a new and execrable type of criminal. It was not long before the appropriate criminal arrived. The scene of the first appearance was the suburb of Tottenham, where two Russian Poles attempted, and failed in, an idiotic street robbery. The attempt was made in broad daylight in the open street, and the two wretches, having failed, ran away, shooting at every human being they met. In the end they were both killed—one by his own hand—but not until they had murdered a gallant constable and a poor little child and injured in all, twenty-two persons.

"I read the newspaper account with deep interest and the conviction that this was only a beginning. Those two frenzied degenerates belonged to a common enough type; the type of the Slav criminal who has not sense enough to take precautions nor courage enough to abide the fortune of war. The automatic pistol, I felt sure, would bring him into view; and I was not mistaken.

"One night, returning from a tour of inspection, I met a small excited crowd accompanying a procession of three police ambulances. I joined the throng and presently turned into a small blind thoroughfare in which had gathered a small and nervous-looking crowd and a few flurried policemen. Several of the windows were shattered and on the ground were three prostrate figures. One was dead, the others were badly wounded, and all three were members of the police force.

"I watched the ambulances depart with their melancholy burdens and then turned for information to a bystander. He had not much to give, but the substance of his account—confirmed later by the newspapers—was this: The police had located a gang of suspected burglars and three officers had come to the house to make arrests. They had knocked at the door, which, after some delay, was opened. Some person within had immediately shot one of the officers dead and the entire gang of four or five had rushed out, fired point blank at the other two officers, and then raced up the street shooting right and left like madmen. Several people had been wounded and, grievous to relate, the whole gang of miscreants had made their escape into the surrounding slums.

"I was profoundly interested and even excited for several reasons. In the first place, here at last was the real Lombroso criminal, the sub-human mattoid, devoid of intelligence, devoid of the faintest glimmering of moral sense, fit for nothing but the lethal chamber; compared with whom the British 'habitual' was a civilized gentleman. Without a specimen or two of this type, my collection was incomplete. Then there was the evident applicability of my methods to this class of offender; methods of quiet extermination without fuss, public disorder or risk to the precious lives of the police. But beyond these there was another reason for my interest. The murder of my wife had been a purposeless, unnecessary crime, committed by some wretch to whom human life was a thing of no consideration. There was an analogy in the circumstances that seemed to connect that murder with this type of miscreant. It was

95

even possible that one of these very villains might be the one whom I had so patiently sought through the long and weary years.

"The thought fired me with a new enthusiasm. Forthwith I started to pursue the possible course of the fugitives, threading countless by-streets and alleys, peering into squalid courts and sending many a doubtful-looking loiterer shuffling hastily round the nearest corner. Of course it was fruitless. I had no clue and did not even know the men. I was merely walking off my own excitement.

"Nevertheless, every night as soon as I had closed my shop, I set forth on a voyage of exploration, impelled by sheer restlessness; and during the day I listened eagerly to the talk of my customers in Yiddish—a language of which I was supposed to be entirely ignorant. But I learned nothing. Either the fugitives were unknown, or the natural secretiveness of an alien people forbade any reference to them, even among themselves; and meanwhile, as I have said, I tramped the streets nightly into the small hours of the morning.

"Returning from one of these expeditions a little earlier than usual, I found a small party of policemen and a sprinkling of idlers gathered opposite the house next door. There was no need to ask what was doing. The suppressed excitement of the officers and the service revolvers in their belts told the story. There was going to be another slaughter; and I was probably too late for any but a spectator's part.

"The street door was open and the house was being quietly emptied of its human occupants. They came out one by one, shivering and complaining, with little bundles of their possessions hastily snatched up, and collected in a miserable group on the pavement. I opened my shop door and invited them to come in and rest while their messengers went to look for a harbor of refuge; but I stayed outside to see the upshot of the proceedings.

"When the last of the tenants had come out, a sergeant emerged and quietly closed the street door with a latch-key. The rest of the policemen took up sheltered positions in doorways after warning the idlers to disperse and the sergeant turned to me.

"'Now, Mr. Vosper, you'd better keep your nose indoors if

you don't want it shot off. There's going to be trouble presently.' He pushed me gently into the shop and shut the door after me.

"I found the evicted tenants chattering excitedly and very unhappy. But they were not rebellious. They were mostly Jews, and Jews are a patient, submissive people. I boiled some water in my little copper and made some coffee, which they drank gratefully — out of shaving mugs; my outfit of crockery being otherwise rather limited. And meanwhile they talked volubly and I listened.

"'I vunder,' said a stout, elderly Jewess, 'how der bolice know dose shentlemens gom to lotch mit me. Zumpotty must haf toldt dem.'

"'Yus,' agreed an evicted tenant of doubtful occupation, 'some bloomin' nark has giv 'em away. Good job too. Tain't playin' the game for to go pottin' at the coppers like that there. Coppers 'as got their job to do same as what we 'ave. You know that, Mrs. Kosminsky.'

"'Ja, dat is droo,' said the Jewess; 'but dey might let me bring my dings mit me. Do-morrow is Ky-fox-tay. Now I lose my money.'

"'How is that, Mrs. Kosminsky?' I asked.

"'Pecause I shall sell dem not, de dings vot I buy for Ky-fox-tay; de fireworks, de gragers, de masgs and oder dings vor de chiltrens. Dvendy-vaive shillings vort I buy. Dey are in my room on ze zecond floor. I ask de bolice to let me vetch dem, hot dey say no; I shall disturb de chentlemens in de front room. Zo I lose my money pecause I sell dem not.' Here the unfortunate woman burst into tears and I was so much affected by her distress that I instantly offered to buy the whole consignment for two pounds, whereat she wept more copiously than ever, but collected the purchase-money with great promptitude and stowed it away in a very internal pocket, displaying in the process as many layers of clothing as an old-fashioned pen-wiper.

"'Ach! Mizder Fosper, you are zo coot to all de boor beebles, dough you are only a boor man yourzelf. Bot it is de boor vot is de vriendts of de boor;' and in her gratitude she would have kissed my hands if I had not prudently stuck them in my trousers pockets.

"A messenger now arrived to say that a refuge had been secured for the night, and my guests departed with many thanks and benedictions. The street, as I looked out, was now quite deserted save for one or two prowling policemen, who, apparently bored with their hiding-places, had come forth to patrol in the open. I did not stay to watch them, for Mrs. Kosminsky's remarks had started a train of thought which required to be carried out quickly. Accordingly I went in and fell to pacing the empty shop.

"The police, I assumed, were waiting for daylight to rush the house. It was a mad plan and yet I was convinced that they had no other. And when they should enter, in the face of a stream of bullets from those terrible automatic pistols, what a carnage there would be! It was frightful to think of. Why does the law permit those cowards' tools to be made and sold? A pistol is the one weapon that has no legitimate use. An axe, a knife—even a rifle, has some lawful function. But a pistol is an appliance for killing human beings. It has no other purpose whatever. A man who is found with house-breaking tools in his possession is assumed to be a house-breaker. Surely a man who carries a pistol convicts himself of the intention to kill somebody.

"But perhaps the police had some reasonable plan. It was possible, but it was very unlikely. The British policeman is a grand fellow, brave as a lion and ready to march cheerfully into the mouth of hell if duty calls. But he knows no tactics. His very courage is almost a disadvantage, leading him to disdain reasonable caution. I felt that our guardians were again going to sacrifice themselves to these vermin. It was terrible. It was a wicked waste of precious lives. Could nothing be done to prevent it?

"According to Mrs. Kosminsky, the 'chentlemens' were in the second floor front—the room with the sliding panel. Then I could, at least, keep a watch on them. I walked slowly upstairs gnashing my teeth with irritation. The sacrifice was so unnecessary. I could think, offhand, of half a dozen ways of annihilating these wretches without risking a single hair of any decent person's head. And here were the police, with all the resources of science at their disposal and practically unlimited time in which to work, actually contemplating a fight with all the odds against them!

"I stole into the second floor front and, by the light of a match, found the cupboard. The inside panel—as I will call the one on my

98

side—slid back without a sound. There was now only the second panel between me and the next room, and I could plainly hear the murmur of voices and sounds of movement. But I could not distinguish what was being said; and as this was of some importance, I determined to try the other panel. Grasping the handle, I gave a firm but gradual pull, and felt the panel slide back quite silently for a couple of inches. Instantly the voices became perfectly distinct and a whiff of foul, stuffy air came through, with a faint glimmer of light; by which I knew that the cupboard on their side was at least partly open.

"'I tell you, Piragoff,' a voice said in Russian, 'you are nervous about nothing. The police are looking for us, but they know none of us by sight. We can go about quite safely.'

"'I am not so sure,' replied another voice—presumably Piragoff's. 'The babbling fool who let us the house may talk more; and who knows but some of our own people may betray us. That woman Kosminsky looked very queerly at us, I thought.'

"'Bah!' exclaimed the other. 'Come and lie down, Piragoff. Tomorrow we will leave this place and separate. We shall go away for a time and they will forget us. Put some more coke in the stove and let us go to sleep.'

"How incalculable are the groupings of factors that evolve the causation of events! Those last words of the invisible ruffian seemed quite trivial and inconsequent; and yet they framed his death warrant. I did not myself realize it fully at the moment. As I closed the slide and stepped back, I was conscious only that a useful train of thought had been started. 'Put some more coke in the stove and let us go to sleep.' Yes; there was a clear connection between the idea of 'stove' and that of 'sleep,' a sleep of infinite duration. Therein lay the solution of the problem.

"I walked slowly down the stairs tracing the connection between the ideas of 'stove' and 'sleep.' The nauseous air that had filtered through from that room spoke eloquently of sealed windows and stopped crevices. It was a frosty night and the murderers were chilly. A back-draught in the stovepipe would fill the room with poisonous gases and probably suffocate these wretches slowly and quietly. But how was it to be brought about?

For a moment I thought of climbing to the roof and stopping the chimney from above. But the plan was a bad one. The police might see me and make some regrettable mistake with a revolver. Besides it would probably fail. The stoppage of the draught would extinguish the fire and the pungent coke-fumes would warn the villains of their danger. Still closely pursuing the train of thought, I stepped into my bedroom and lit the gas; I turned to glance round the room; and, behold! the problem was solved.

"In the fireplace stood a little brass stove of Russian make; a tiny affair, too small to burn anything but charcoal; but, as charcoal was easily obtainable in East London, I had bought it and fixed it myself. It was perfectly safe in a well-ventilated room, though otherwise very dangerous; for the fumes of charcoal, consisting of nearly pure carbon dioxide, being practically inodorous, give no warning.

"My course was now quite clear. The stove was fitted with asbestos-covered handles; a box of charcoal stood by the hearth, and in the corner was an extra length of stovepipe for which I had had no use. But I had a use for it now.

"I lit the charcoal in the stove, and, while it was burning up, carried the stovepipe and the box of fuel upstairs. Then I returned for the stove, inside which the charcoal was now beginning to glow brightly. I fixed on the extra length of pipe and, with my hand, felt the stream of hot air—or rather hot carbon dioxide gas—pouring out of its mouth. I tried the pipe against the opening and found that it would rest comfortably on the lower edge; and then, very slowly and cautiously, I drew back the sliding panel about six inches. The ruffians were still wrangling on the same subject, for I heard one exclaim:

"'Don't be a fool, Piragoff. You'll only attract attention if you go nosing about downstairs.'

"'I don't care,' was the answer; 'I feel uneasy. I must go down and see that all is quiet before I go to sleep.' Here the sound of the opening and shutting of the door put an end to the discussion, save for a torrent of curses and maledictions from the two remaining men. But in a few moments the door opened noisily and Piragoff shouted:

"'Come out! Come out! The house is empty! We are betrayed.'

"A howl of dismay was the answer. The two wretches burst into a grotesque mixture of weeping and cursing, and I heard them literally dancing about the room in the ecstasy of their terror.

"'Come out!' repeated Piragoff. 'We will kill them all! We will shoot those pigs, every one of them! Some of us shall get away. Come!'

"'It is of no use, Piragoff,' whimpered one of his comrades. 'They are in the house. It is an ambush.'

"'Yes,' cried the third man, 'it is as Boris says. The house is dark and they are hiding in it. Bolt the door and let them come up to us; and we will kill them—kill!—kill!—kill!' he ended with an unearthly shriek and a burst of hysterical sobs.

"'I shall go,' said Piragoff. 'There is a chance.'

"'There is none,' shrieked the other. 'Come back, madman!'

"The door slammed, the key turned in the lock and a heavy bolt was shot. I quietly closed the slide and ran down to the open window of the first floor front room.

"The street appeared to be empty save for two constables who stood at a corner conversing in low tones. A profound silence reigned—an unusual silence, as it seemed!—through which the subdued murmur of the constables' voices was faintly audible. I looked out anxiously, debating whether I ought not to warn the unconscious sentinels even at the risk of defeating my plans. Suddenly two sharp reports in quick succession rang out from below; both constables fell, and a figure darted out of the doorway and raced madly up the street.

"One of the fallen constables lay motionless; the other grasped his hip with one hand and with the other fired his revolver repeatedly at the retreating murderer, but apparently missed him every time. In a few seconds a sergeant and another constable came flying round the corner; police whistles began to sound their warning in all directions; and the previous silence gave place to a very Babel of noise. But Piragoff had shot up a side turning before the sergeant arrived, and the persistent clamor of the whistles told me that he had, for the moment, at least, escaped. I turned away.

Piragoff was out of my hands, and what I had seen only made it more imperative that I should prevent further bloodshed.

"As, once more, I softly opened the slide, the voices of the miserable wretches within came to me in a strange and unpleasant mixture of curses, blasphemies and hysterical sobs. They cursed Piragoff, they cursed the police, they invoked death and destruction on every man, woman and child in this nation of pigs; and between the curses they wept and lamented. I had shut the damper of the stove before going down, but the charcoal was still alight, though dull. I now arranged the stove in position, resting the long pipe on the bottom edge of the opening so that its end projected a few inches into the room; moving quite silently and assisted by the hubbub from without and the noise produced by the two craven villains. When it was fixed, I opened the damper, and presently, holding my hand opposite the mouth of the pipe, felt a strong current of hot gas pouring out. That gas would cool rapidly on meeting the cold air, and then would fall by its own weight and collect about the floor.

"My apparatus was now in full going order and there was nothing for it but to wait. The noise in the street had subsided, but the two ruffians showed no signs of settling down. They were now engaged in barricading the door so that it could be forced open only a few inches, thus exposing the attackers to a deadly fire. I was much obliged to them. Their movements would help to diffuse the gas and prevent it from settling too densely on the floor. Also, their exertions would make them breathe more deeply and so come more rapidly under the influence of the poison.

"The time crept on; the police made no sign; the murderers rested from their labors, sometimes talking excitedly, sometimes silent for minutes at a time, and at intervals yawning like overstrung women. And all the time the invisible stream of heavy, deadly gas was pouring out of the stovepipe and trickling unseen along the floor. Even now it must be eddying about the murderers' feet and slowly diffusing upwards. If only the police would remain quiescent for an hour or two more, the danger would be over.

"The long hours of the winter's night dragged out their weary length. Yet not weary to me. For, as I kept my vigil by the pipe and fed the stove silently at intervals, I was on the very tip-toe of expectation. Every moment I dreaded to hear the disastrous crash on the door that should herald a fresh slaughter; and, as the minutes passed and all remained still, hope rose higher and higher. Sometimes I caught a glimpse of my quarry through the chink of their cupboard door; for I had opened the slide fully a foot, finding that the clothes that hung from the pegs would screen me, even if the darkness on my side had not done so already. So I saw one of them sit down on a low chair and crouch, shuddering, over the coke stove, while the other restlessly paced the room.

"And still the stream of deadly gas trickled unceasingly from the pipe.

"Presently the former rose and yawned heavily. 'Bah!' he growled, 'I am tired. I shall lie down. If I fall asleep, Boris, do you watch, and wake me if you hear them coming.'

"By craning my neck through the opening I could just continue to get a glimpse of him as he threw himself on a mattress that was spread on the floor. The other man continued for a while to pace the room; then he sat down on the chair and spread his hands out over the stove, muttering to himself. I watched him as well as I could through the chink of the cupboard doors by the dim light of the stinking paraffin lamp; a greasy, unwholesome-looking wretch, sallow, pallid and unshorn; and thought how striking he would look in the form of a reduced, dry preparation.

"But that was impossible. I was now working only for the police. Regrettable as it was, I should have to surrender these two specimens to the coroner and the gravedigger. A deplorable waste of material, but unavoidable—even if one of them should prove to be my long-sought enemy.

"At this thought I started; and at that moment the man on the mattress gave a strange, snorting cry. The ruffian, Boris, looked round, rose, went over to the mattress and stirred the other with his foot. 'Louis! Louis!' he cried angrily, 'what the devil are you making that noise for?'

"The other man scrambled up with a cry of terror, pistol in hand. 'Ah! it is you, Boris! I was dreaming. I thought they had come.' He sat down again on the mattress and yawned. 'Bah! I am sleepy. I must lie down again. Watch a little longer, Boris.'

"'Why should I watch?' demanded Boris. 'They will make enough noise opening that door. I shall lie down a little, too.'

"He flung himself down beside his comrade, but in a minute or two started up, taking deep breaths. 'My God!' he exclaimed. 'I can't breathe lying down. I feel as if I should choke. And you, too, Louis; you are snoring like a pig. Get up, man.'

"He shook the prostrate man roughly, but eliciting only a few drowsy curses, resumed his restless pacing of the room. But not for long. Yawn after yawn told me that the gas was already in his blood; and the loud snoring of the other man indicated plainly the state of the air in the lower part of the room. Presently Boris halted in his walk and sat down by the stove, muttering as before. Soon he began to nod; then he nearly fell forward on the stove. Finally he rose heavily, staggered across to the mattress and once more flung himself down.

"I breathed more freely, notwithstanding that the gas, having partially diffused upwards to the level of the opening, now began to filter through to my side. I waited a minute or two listening to the breathing of the two murderers as it grew moment by moment more stertorous and irregular, and then, having filled up the stove, went down to the first floor and sat awhile by the open window to breathe the relatively fresh air.

"All was now quiet in the street. No doubt the guard had been strengthened, but I did not look out. It was as well not to be seen at that hour in the morning. As I sat by the window, I thought about the two men in that deadly room. It was a thousand pities that they should be lost to science. Yet there was no help for it. Even if I had decided to acquire them I could not have done so, for, by the very worst of luck, I had used up my last barrel and had neglected to lay in a fresh stock. Besides, of course, the police knew they were there.

"I rested for half an hour or so and then went upstairs to see how matters were progressing. No light now came through the opening in the wall, for the paraffin lamp had either burned out or been extinguished by the accumulating gas. I listened attentively.

The harsh, metallic ticking of a cheap American clock was plainly, even intrusively, audible; otherwise no sound came from that chamber of death.

"I drew the sliding panel right back, held aside the dangling garments, and, climbing through into the cupboard, pushed open the doors. A faint glimmer of light from the street made dimly visible the mattress on the floor and two indistinct dark shapes stretched on it. I stepped quickly across the room, breathing as little as possible of the unspeakably foul air, and struck a wax match. It burned dimly and smokily, but showed me the two murderers, lying in easy postures, their faces livid and ghastly in hue but peaceful enough in expression. When I lowered the match, its flame dwindled and turned blue, and at eighteen inches from the floor it went out as if dipped in water. At that height the heavy gas must have been nearly pure. The room was a veritable Grotto del Cane.

"I stooped quickly, holding my breath, and felt the wrists of the two men. They were chilly to the touch and no vestige of pulse was perceptible. I shook them both vigorously, but failed to elicit any responsive movement. They were quite limp and inert and I had no doubt that they were dead. My work was done. The policemen were now safe, whatever follies they might commit; and it only remained for me to remove the traces of the fairy godmother who had labored through the night to save them from their own exuberant courage.

"Passing back through the opening, I drew away the now unnecessary pipe, closed the two panels, and carried the little stove down to my bedroom. I looked at the unruffled bed—mute but eloquent witness to the night's activity—and deciding as a measure of prudence to give it the appearance of having been slept in, took off my boots and crept in between the sheets. But I was not in the least degree drowsy. Quite the contrary. I was all agog to see the end of the comedy in which I had, all unknown, taken the leading part; so that after tossing about for a few minutes I sprang out of bed, resumed my boots and poured out a basin full of water to refresh myself by a wash.

"And now once more observe the strangely indirect lines of causation. The towels on the horse were damp and none too clean. I flung them into the dirty-linen basket and dragged open the drawer in which the clean ones were kept. It was the bottom drawer of a cheap pine chest that I had bought in Whitechapel High Street. That chest of drawers was of unusual size; it was four feet wide by nearly five feet high, and the two bottom drawers were each fully eighteen inches deep, and were far larger than was necessary for my modest stock of household linen.

"I pulled out the bottom drawer, then, and as its great cavity yawned before me, it offered a not unnatural suggestion. The length of an average man's head and trunk is under thirty-six inches. Allowing a few inches more for his feet and ankles, a cavity forty-eight inches long is amply sufficient for his accommodation. Flinging out the towels and sheets that lay in the drawer, I got in and lay down with my knees drawn up. Of course there was room and to spare.

"It was an interesting fact but not very applicable to present circumstances. Still, it set me thinking. I went into the front room and glanced out of the open window. A faint lightening of the murky sky heralded the approach of dawn, and from afar came the murmur of commencing traffic out in High Street. I was about to turn away when my ear caught a new and unusual sound rising above that distant murmur; the measured tread of feet mingling with the clatter of horses' hoofs and a heavy, metallic rumbling. I looked out cautiously in the direction whence the sounds came and was positively stupefied with amazement. At the end of the street I saw, by the light of the lamps, a company of soldiers appearing round the corner and taking up a position across the road. I watched breathlessly. Soon, at a sign from the officer, the men spread mats on the muddy ground and lay down on them, and then appeared a train of horses, dragging a field-piece or quick-firing gun, which was halted behind the infantry and unlimbered. A minute later the black shapes of a number of soldiers appeared on the sky-line as they crept along the parapets of the opposite houses where, save for their heads and the barrels of their rifles, they presently disappeared.

"It seemed that I had misjudged the police in the matter of caution. It almost seemed that my labors had been useless; for surely these portentous preparations indicated some masterpiece of strategy. What an anticlimax it would be when the defenders of the fort were found to be dead! But what a still greater anticlimax if they were not there at all!

"At this moment a police sergeant strolled down the middle of the road and, observing me, motioned to me with his hand to get inside out of harm's way. I obeyed with grim amusement, thinking of that absurd anticlimax; and somehow this idea began to connect itself with those two bottom drawers. But the casks were the difficulty. The cooper from whom I had obtained them sometimes kept me waiting nearly a week before supplying them—for I was only a small customer; and that would never do even at this time of year. Besides, the police would make a rigid search; not that that would have mattered if I could have made proper arrangements for the concealment and removal of the specimens. But unfortunately I could not. The specimens would have to go; to be borne out ingloriously in the face of the besieging force, limp and passive, like a couple of those very helpless guys that are wont to be produced by what Mrs. Kosminsky would call 'der chiltrens.' There would be a certain grim appropriateness in the incident. For this was the fifth of November.

"The generation of new ideas is chiefly a matter of association. The ideas 'guys,' 'Mrs. Kosminsky' and 'the fifth of November' unconsciously formed themselves into a group from which in an instant there was evolved a new and startling train of thought. At first it seemed wild enough; but when the two bottom drawers joined in the synthetic process, a complete and consistent scheme began to appear. A flush of pleasurable excitement swept over me, and as I raced upstairs fresh details added themselves and fresh difficulties were propounded and disposed of. I slid open the panels, stepped through and, holding my breath, strode across the poisoned room with only one quick glance at the two still forms on the mattress. Removing the barricading chair, I unlocked and unbolted the door and passed out, closing it after me.

"Mrs. Kosminsky's room was at the back; a dreadful nest of dirt and squalor, piled almost to the ceiling with unclassifiable rubbish. The air was so stifling that I was tempted to raise the

107

heavily-curtained window a couple of inches; and thereby got a useful idea when, by peeping over the curtain, I saw the flat leads of a projecting lower story. The merchandise piled on all sides, and even under the bed, included very secondhand wearing apparel, sheets, blankets, crockery and toys. Among them were the fireworks, the masks and other appliances for commemorating the never-to-be-forgotten 'Gunpowder treason,' and a couple of large balls of a dark-colored cord sometimes used by costers for securing their loads. That gave me an idea, too, as did the frowsily-smart female garments. I appropriated four of the largest masks and a quantity of oakum for wigs; some colored-paper streamers and hat-frills; two huge and disreputable dresses—Mrs. Kosminsky's own, I suspected—the skirts of which I crammed with straw from a hamper; two large-sized and ragged suits of clothes, a woman's straw hat, four pairs of men's gloves and the biggest top-hat that I could find. These I put apart in a heap with one of the balls of cord. From the other ball I cut off some eight fathoms of cord, and, poking it out through the opening of the window, let it drop on the leads beneath. Then I conveyed my spoil in one or two journeys across the murderers' room, passed it through the opening, and closed the panel after me.

"Prudence suggested that I should dispose of these things first, and accordingly I stowed two masks, two pairs of gloves, one suit of clothes and one dress in the large chest of drawers. The rest I carried down to the back yard, where already was a quantity of lumber belonging to a neighboring green grocer. Returning upstairs, I called in at the bedroom to transfer the scanty contents of the two large drawers into the upper ones and then proceeded once more to the second floor front. Time was passing and the glimmer of the gray dawn was beginning to struggle in faintly through the dirty windows.

"As I drew back the slide I became aware of a sound which, soft as it was, rang the knell of my newly-formed hopes. I had closed the door of the murderers' room and locked it, but had not shot the bolt. Now I could distinctly hear someone fumbling gently at the keyhole, apparently with a picklock. It was most infuriating. At the very last moment, when success was within my grasp, I was to be foiled and all my neatly-laid plans defeated. And to make it a thousand times worse, I had not even taken the precaution to examine the dead miscreants' hair!

"With an angry and foolish exclamation, I reached through the opening and drew the cupboard doors to, leaving only a small chink. Then I shut myself in my own cupboard, to exclude the dim light, and closing the panel to within an inch, waited on events with my hand on the knob, ready to shut it at a moment's notice. The great strategic move was about to begin and I was curious to see what it would be.

"The bolt of the lock shot back; the door creaked softly. There was a pause, and then a voice whispered:

"'Why, they seem to be asleep! Keep them covered, Smith, and shoot if they move.'

"Soft footsteps advanced across the room. Someone gave a choking cough and then a brassy voice fairly shouted, 'Why, man, they're dead! My Lord! What a let-off!'

"An unsteady laugh told of the effort it had cost the worthy officer to take this frightful risk.

"'Yes,' said another voice, 'they're dead enough. They've cheated us after all. Not that I complain of that. But, my eye, sir; what a sell! Think of all those Tommies and that machine gun. Ha! ha! Oh! Lord! I suppose the beggars poisoned themselves when they saw the game was up.' He laughed again and the laugh ended in a fit of coughing.

"'Not they, Sergeant,' said the other. 'It was that coke stove that gave them their ticket. Can't you smell it? And, by Jove, it will give us our ticket if we don't clear out. We'll just run down and report and send for a couple of stretchers.'

"'Hadn't I better wait here, sir, while you're gone?' asked the sergeant.

"'Lord, no, man. What for? We shall want three stretchers if you do. Come along. Pooh! Leave the door open.'

"I listened incredulously to their retreating footsteps. It seemed hardly possible that they should be so devoid of caution. And yet, why not? The men were dead. And dead men are not addicted to sudden disappearances.

109

"But this case was going to be an exception. I had given the specimens up for lost when I heard the police enter; but now —

"I opened the slide, sprang through the opening, and strode over to the mattress. One after the other, I picked up the prostrate ruffians, carried them across and bundled them through the aperture. Then I came through myself, shut the cupboard doors, closed both panels carefully, shut up my own cupboard and carried the specimens down to my bedroom. With their knees drawn up, they packed quite easily in the large drawers. I shut them in, locked the drawers, pocketed the key, washed my hands and went down to the parlor, where I rapidly laid the breakfast table. At any moment now, the police might come to inspect, and whenever they came, they would find me ready.

"I did not waste time on breakfast. That could wait. Meanwhile I fell to work with the materials in the yard. In addition to the hand-cart, there was now a coster's barrow, the property of a greengrocer, to whom also belonged a quantity of lumber, including some bundles of stakes and several hampers filled with straw. With these materials, and those that I had borrowed from Mrs. Kosminsky, I began rapidly to build up a pair of life-sized guys—one male and one female. I put them together very roughly and sat them side by side in the barrow, leaning against the wall; and to each I attached a large ticket on which I had scrawled the name of the person it represented; one being the highly unpopular minister, Mr. Todd-Leeks, and the other the notorious Mrs. Gamway.

"They were very sketchily built and would have dropped to pieces at a touch. But that was of no consequence. The time factor was the important one; and I had worked at such speed that I had huddled them into a pretty plausible completeness when the inevitable peal at the house bell disturbed my labors. I darted into the parlor, crammed a piece of bread into my mouth and rushed out to the shop door, chewing frantically. As I opened the door, an agitated police inspector burst in, followed by a sergeant.

"'Good morning, gentlemen,' I said suavely. 'Hair-cutting or shaving?'

"I shall not record the inspector's reply. I was really shocked. I

110

had no idea that responsible officials used such language. In effect, they wished to look over the premises. Of course I gave instant permission, and followed them in their tour of inspection on the pretext of showing them over the house.

"The inspector was in a very bad temper and the sergeant was obviously depressed. They conversed in low tones as they stumped up the stairs and I heard the sergeant say something about 'an awful suck in.'

"'Oh, don't talk of it,' snapped the inspector. 'It's enough to make a cat sick. But what beats me is how those devils could have stuck the air of that room. It would have settled my hash in five minutes.'

"'Yes,' agreed the sergeant; 'and how they could have let themselves down from that window without being spotted. I wouldn't have believed it if I hadn't seen the cord. The constables must have been asleep.'

"'Yes,' grunted the inspector; 'thickheaded louts. Let's have a look out here.' He strode into the second floor back and threw up the window. 'Now you see,' he continued, 'what I mean. This house has no connection with the next one. That projecting wing cuts it off. This back yard opens into Bell's Alley; the yard next door opens into Kosher Court. That's the way they went. They couldn't have got to this house excepting by the roof, and we've seen that they went down, not up.' He stuck his head out of the window and looked down sourly at the guys.

"'Those things yours?' he asked gruffly, pointing at the effigies.

"'No,' I answered. 'I think one of Piper's men is getting them ready to take round.'

"The inspector grunted and moved away. He walked into the front room, looked in the cupboard, glanced round and went downstairs. On the first floor, he made a perfunctory inspection of the rooms, glancing in at my bedroom, and then went down to the ground floor. From thence the two officers descended to the cellar, which they examined more thoroughly, even prodding the sawdust in the bin, and so up to the back yard. Here, at the sight of the guys, the sergeant's woeful countenance brightened somewhat.

111

"'Ha!' he exclaimed; 'Mrs. Gamway! I saw a good deal of her when I was in the Westminster division. I've often thought I'd like to—and, by Jimini! I will!' He squared up fiercely at the helpless-looking effigy of the lady, and, with a vicious, round-arm punch, sent its unstable head flying across the yard.

"The blow and its effect seemed to rouse his destructive instincts, for he returned to the attack with such ferocity that in a few seconds he had reduced, not only the factitious Mrs. Gamway, but the Right Honorable Todd-Leeks also, to a heap of ruin.

"'Stop that foolery, Smith,' snarled the inspector; 'you'll give the poor devil the trouble of building them up all over again. Come along.' He unlocked the gate and stood for a moment looking back at me.

"'I suppose you've heard nothing in the night?' he said.

"'Not a sound,' I answered, adding, 'I shan't open the shop until the evening, and I shall probably go out for the day. Would you like to have the key?'

"The inspector shook his head. 'No, I don't want the key. I've seen all I want to see. Good morning,' and he stumped out, followed by his subordinate.

"I drew a deep breath as I re-locked the gate. I was glad he had refused the key, though I had thought it prudent to make the offer. Now I was at liberty to complete my arrangements at leisure.

"My first proceeding, after locking up the shop, was to rig up, with the green grocer's stakes and Mrs. Kosminsky's cord, a firm pair of standards to support the guys. Then I took a hearty breakfast, after which I repaired to my bedroom with a hamper of straw, a bundle of small stakes and a quantity of odd rags. The process of converting the specimens into quite convincing guys was not difficult. Tying up the heads in large pieces of rag, I fastened the big masks to the fronts of the globular bundles and covered in the remainder with masses of oakum to form appropriate wigs. Each figure was then clothed in the bulky garments borrowed from Mrs. Kosminsky's stock and well stuffed with straw, portions of which I allowed to protrude at all the apertures. A suitable stiffness was imparted to the limbs by pieces of stick poked up inside the clothing, and smaller sticks gave the correct, starfish-like spread to

112

the gloved hands. When they were finished, the illusion was perfect. As the two effigies sat on the floor with their backs against the wall, stiff, staring, bloated and grotesquely horrible, not a soul would have suspected them.

"I carried the male guy down to the yard, sat him on the barrow and put on his hat; and taking with me the remains of the ruined guys, which I decided to put away in the drawers, I returned for the second effigy. I lashed the two figures very securely to the standards, fixed on their hats firmly, and attached their name-cards. Then I went into the shop to attend to my own appearance.

"I had brought back from my Bloomsbury house the shabby overcoat and battered hat that I had worn on the last few expeditions. These I now assumed; and having fixed on my cheek a large cross of sticking-plaster—which pulled down my eyebrow and pulled up the corner of my mouth—begrimed my face, reddened my nose, and carefully tinted in a not too emphatic black eye, I was sufficiently transmogrified to deceive even my intimate friends. Now I was ready to start; and now was the critical moment.

"I went out into the yard, unlocked the gate, trundled the barrow out into the alley, and locked the gate behind me. At the moment there was not a soul in sight, but from the street close by came the unmistakable murmur of a large crowd. I must confess that I felt a little nervous. The next few minutes would decide my fate.

"I grasped the handles of the barrow and started forward resolutely. As I rounded the curve of the alley, a densely-packed throng appeared ahead. Faces turned towards me and broke into grins; the murmur rose into a dull roar, and, as the people drew aside to make way for me, I plunged into the heart of the throng and raised my voice in a husky chant:

> "'Remember, remember the Fifth of November,
> The Gunpowder Treason and Plot.'

"Through the interstices of the crowd I could see the soldiers still drawn up by the curb and even the machine gun was yet in position. Suddenly the inspector and the sergeant appeared bustling through the crowd. The former caught sight of me and, waving his hand angrily, shouted:

"'Take that thing away from here! Move him out of the crowd, Moloney;' and a gigantic constable pounced on me with a broad grin, snatched the barrow-handles out of my hands, and started off at a trot that made the effigies rock in the most alarming manner.

"'Holler, bhoys!' shouted the grinning constable; and the 'bhoys' complied with raucous enthusiasm.

"At the outskirts of the crowd Constable Moloney resigned in my favor, and it was at this moment that I noticed a manifest plain-clothes officer observing my exhibits with undue attention. But here fortune favored me; for at the same instant I saw a man attempt to pick a pocket under the officer's very nose. The pickpocket caught my eye and moved off quickly. I pulled up, and, pointing at the thief, bawled out, 'Stop that man! Stop him!' The pickpocket flung himself into the crowd and made off. The startled loafers drew hastily away from him. Men shouted, women screamed, and the plain-clothes officer started in pursuit; and in the whirling confusion that followed, I trundled away briskly into Middlesex Street and headed for Spitalfields.

"My progress through the squalid streets was quite triumphal. A large juvenile crowd attended me, with appropriate vocal music, and adults cheered from the pavements, though no one embarrassed me with gifts. But, for all my outward gaiety, I was secretly anxious. It was barely ten o'clock and many hours of the dreary November day had yet to run before it would be safe for me to approach my destination. The prospect of tramping the streets for some ten or twelve hours with this very conspicuous appendage was far from agreeable, to say nothing of the increasing risk of detection, and I looked forward to it with gloomy forebodings. If a suspicion arose, I could be traced with the greatest ease, and in any case I should be spent with fatigue before evening. Reflecting on these difficulties, I had decided to seek some retired spot where I could dismount the effigies, cover them with the tarpaulin that was rolled up in the barrow and take a rest, when once more circumstances befriended me.

"All through the night and morning the ordinary winter haze

114

had hung over the town; but now, by reason of a change of wind, the haze began rapidly to thicken into a definite fog. I set down the barrow and watched with thankfulness the mass of opaque yellow vapor filling the street and blotting out the sky. As it thickened and the darkness closed in, the children strayed away and only one solitary loafer remained.

""'Ard luck for you, mate, this 'ere fog,' he remarked, 'arter you've took all that trouble, too.' (He little knew how much.) 'But it's no go. You'd better git 'ome whilst you can find yer way. This is goin' to be a black 'un.'

"I thanked him for his sympathy and moved on into the darkening vapor. Close to Spital Square I found a quiet corner where I quickly dismounted the guys, covered them with the tarpaulin and, urged by a new anxiety from the rapidly-growing density of the fog, groped my way into Norton Folgate. Here I moved forward as quickly as I dared, turned up Great Eastern Street and at length, to my great relief, came out into Old Street.

"It was none too soon. As I entered the well-known thoroughfare, the fog closed down into impenetrable obscurity. The world of visible objects was extinguished and replaced by a chaos of confused sounds. Even the end of my barrow faded away into spectral uncertainty, and the curb against which I kept my left wheel grinding looked thin and remote.

"Opportune as the fog was, it was not without its dangers; of which the most immediate was that I might lose my way. I set down the barrow, and, detaching the little compass that I always carry on my watch-guard, laid it on the tarpaulin. My course, as I knew, lay about west-southwest, and with the compass before me, I could not go far wrong. Indeed, its guidance was invaluable; without it I could never have found my way through those miles of intricate streets. When a stationary wagon or other obstruction sent me out into the road, it enabled me to pick up the curb again unerringly. It mapped out the corners of intersecting streets, it piloted me over the wide crossings of the City Road and Aldersgate Street, and kept me happily confident of my direction as I groped my way like a fogbound ship on an invisible sea.

"I went as quickly as was safe, but very warily, for a collision

115

might have been fatal. Listening intently, with my eye on the compass and my wheel at the curb, I pushed on through the yellow void until a shadowy post at a street corner revealed itself by its parish initials as that at the intersection of Red Lion Street and Theobald's Row.

"I was nearly home. Another ten minutes' careful navigation brought me to a corner which I believed to be the one opposite my own house. I turned back a dozen paces, put down the barrow and crossed the pavement—with the compass in my hand, lest I should not be able to find the barrow again. I came against the jamb of a street door, I groped across to the door itself, I found the keyhole of the familiar Yale pattern, I inserted my key and turned it; and the door of the museum entrance opened. I had brought my ship into port.

"I listened intently. Someone was creeping down the street, hugging the railings. I closed the door to let him pass, and heard the groping hands sweep over the door as he crawled by. Then I went out, steered across to the barrow, picked up one of the specimens and carried it into the hall, where I laid it on the floor, returning immediately for the other. When both the specimens were safely deposited, I came out, softly closing the door after me with the key, and once more took up the barrow-handles. Slowly I trundled the invaluable little vehicle up the street, never losing touch of the curb, flinging the stakes and cordage into the road as I went, until I had brought it to the corner of a street about a quarter of a mile from my house; and there I abandoned it, making my way back as fast as I could to the museum.

"My first proceeding on my return was to carry my treasures to the laboratory, light the gas and examine their hair. I had really some hopes that one of them might be the man I sought. But, alas! It was the old story. They both had coarse black hair of the mongoloid type. My enemy was still to seek.

"Having cleaned away my 'make-up,' I spent the rest of the day pushing forward the preliminary processes so that these might be completed before 'decay's effacing fingers' should obliterate the details of the integumentary structures. In the evening I returned to Whitechapel and opened the shop, proposing to purchase the dummy skeletons on the following day and to devote the succeeding nights and early mornings to the preparation of the specimens.

"The barrow turned up next day in the possession of an undeniable tramp who was trying to sell it for ten shillings and who was accused of having stolen it but was discharged for want of evidence. I compensated the green grocer for the trouble occasioned by my carelessness in leaving the back gate open; and thus the incident came to an end. With one important exception, for there was a very startling sequel.

"On the day after the expedition, I had the curiosity to open the panels and go through into the room that the murderers had occupied, which had now been locked up by the police. Looking round the room, my eye lighted on a shabby cloth cap lying on the still undisturbed mattress just below the pillow. I picked it up and looked it over curiously, for by its size I could see that it did not belong to either of the men whom I had secured. I took it over to the curtained window and carefully inspected its lining; and suddenly I perceived, clinging to the coarse cloth, a single short hair, which, even to the naked eye, had a distinctly unusual appearance. With a trembling hand, I drew out my lens to examine it more closely; and, as it came into the magnified field, my heart seemed to stand still. For, even at that low magnification, its character was unmistakable—it looked like a tiny string of pale gray beads. Grasping it in my fingers, I dashed through the opening, slammed the panels to, and rushed down to the parlor where I kept a small microscope. My agitation was so intense that I could hardly focus the instrument, but at last the object on the slide came into view: a broad, variegated stripe, with its dark medulla and the little rings of air bubbles at regular intervals. It was a typical ringed hair! And what was the inference?

"The hair was almost certainly Piragoff's. Piragoff was a burglar, a ruthless murderer, and he had ringed hair. The man whom I sought was a burglar, a ruthless murderer, and had ringed hair. Then Piragoff was my man. It was bad logic, but the probabilities were overwhelming. And I had had the villain in the hollow of my hand and he had gone forth unscathed!

117

"I ground my teeth with impotent rage. It was maddening. All the old passion and yearning for retribution surged up in my breast once more. My interest in the new specimens almost died out. I wanted Piragoff; and it was only the new-born hope that I should yet lay my hand on him that carried me through that time of bitter disappointment."

VII

THE UTTERMOST FARTHING

Intense was the curiosity with which I turned to the last entry in Humphrey Challoner's "Museum Archives." Not that I had any doubt as to the issue of the adventure that it recorded. I had seen the specimen numbered "twenty-five" in the shallow box, and its identity had long since been evident. But this fact mitigated my curiosity not at all. The "Archives" had furnished a continuous narrative—surely one of the strangest ever committed to writing—and now I was to read the climax of that romantically terrible story; to witness the final achievement of that object that my poor friend had pursued with such unswerving pertinacity.

I extract the entry entire with the exception of one or two passages near the end, the reasons for the omission of which will be obvious to the reader.

"Circumstances attending the acquirement of the specimen numbered 'twenty-five' in the Anthropological Series (A. Osteology. B. Reduced dry preparations).

"The months that followed the events connected with the acquirement of the specimens 23 and 24 brought me nothing but aching suspense and hope deferred. The pursuit of the common criminal I had abandoned since I had got scent of my real quarry. The concussor lay idle in its basket; the cellar steps were greased no more. I had but a passive rôle to play until the hour should strike to usher in the final scene—if that should ever be. Though the term of my long exile in East London was drawing nigh, its approach was unseen by me. I could but wait; and what is harder than waiting?

"I had made cautious inquiries among the alien population. But no one knew Piragoff—or, at least, admitted any knowledge of him; and as to the police, when they had made a few arrests and then released the prisoners, they appeared to let the matter drop. The newspapers were, of course, more active. One of them described circumstantially how 'the three anarchists who escaped from the house in Saul Street' had been seen together in an East End restaurant; and several others followed from day to day the supposed whereabouts of a mysterious person known as 'Paul the Plumber,' whom the police declared to be a picturesque myth. But for me there was one salient fact: of those three ruffians one was still at large, and no one seemed to have any knowledge of him.

"It was some four months later that I again caught up the scent. A certain Friday evening early in February found me listlessly tidying up the shop; for the Jewish Sabbath had begun and customers were few. But about eight o'clock a man strode in jauntily, hung up his hat and seated himself in the operating chair; and at that moment a second man entered and sat down to wait. I glanced at this latter, and in an instant my gorge rose at him. I cannot tell why. To the scientific mind, intuitions are abhorrent. They are mostly wrong and wholly unreasonable. But as I looked at that man a wave of instinctive dislike and suspicion swept over me. He was, indeed, an ill-looking fellow enough. A broad, lozenge-shaped Tartar face, with great cheekbones and massive jaws; a low forehead surmounted by a dense brush of up-standing grayish-brown hair; beetling brows and eyes deep-set, fierce and furtive; combined to make a sufficiently unprepossessing countenance. Nor was his manner more pleasing. He scowled forbiddingly at me, he scrutinized the other customer, craning sideways to survey him in the mirror, he looked about the shop and he stared inquisitively at the parlor door. Every movement was expressive of watchful, uneasy suspicion.

"I tried to avoid looking at him lest my face should betray me, and, to divert my thoughts, concentrated my attention on the other customer. The latter unconsciously gave me every assistance in doing so. Though by no means a young man, he was the vainest and most dandified client I had ever had under my hands. He stopped me repeatedly to give exhaustive directions as to the effect that he desired me to produce. He examined himself in the glass and consulted me anxiously as to the exact disposition of an artificially curled forelock. I cursed him inwardly, for I wanted him to be gone and leave me alone with the other man, but for that very reason and that I might conceal my impatience, I did his bidding and treated him with elaborate care. But now and again my glance would stray to the other man; and as I caught his fierce, suspicious eye—like the eye of a hunted animal—I would look away quickly lest he should read what was in my mind.

"At length I had finished my dandy client. I had brushed his hair to a nicety and had even curled his forelock with heated tongs. With a sigh of relief I took off the cloth and waited for him to rise. But he rose not. Stroking his cheek critically he decided that he wanted shaving, and, cursing him in my heart, I had to comply.

"I had acquired some reputation as a barber and, I think, deserved it. I could put a perfect edge on a razor and I wielded the instrument with a sensitive hand and habitual care. My client appreciated my skill and complimented me patronizingly in very fair English, though with a slight Russian accent, delaying me intolerably to express his approval. When I had shaved him he asked for pink powder to be applied to his chin; and when I had powdered him he directed me to shape his mustache with Pate Hongrois, a process which he superintended with anxious care.

"At last the fellow was actually finished. He got up from the chair and surveyed himself in the large wall-mirror. He turned his head from side to side and tried to see the back of it. He smiled into the mirror, raised his eyebrows, frowned and, in fact, tried a variety of expressions and effects, including a slight and graceful bow. Then he approached the glass to examine a spot on his cheek; leaned against it with outspread hands to inspect his teeth, and finally put out his tongue to examine that too. I almost expected that he would ask me to brush it. However, he did not. Adjusting his necktie delicately, he handed me my fee with a patronizing smile and remarked, 'You are a good barber: you have taste and you take trouble. I give you a penny for yourself and I shall come to you again.'

"As the door closed behind him I turned to the other customer. He rose, walked over to the operating chair and sat down sullenly, keeping an eye on me all the time; and something in his face expressive of suspicion, uneasiness and even fear seemed to hint at something unusual in my own appearance.

"It was likely enough. Hard as I had struggled to smother the tumult of emotions that seethed within me, some disturbance must have reached the surface, some light in the eye, some tension of the mouth to tell of the fierce excitement, the raging anxiety, that possessed me. I was afraid to look at him for fear of frightening him away.

"Was he the man? Was this the murderer, Piragoff, the slayer of my wife? The question rang in my ears as, with a far from steady hand, I slowly lathered his face. Instinct told me that he was. But, even in my excitement, reason rejected a mere unanalyzable belief. For what is an intuition? Brutally stated, it is simply a conclusion reached without premises. I had always disbelieved in instinct and intuition and I disbelieved still. But what had made me connect this man with Piragoff? He was clearly a Russian. He looked like a villain. He had the manner of a Nihilist or violent criminal of some kind. But all this was nothing. It formed no rational basis for the conviction that possessed me.

"There was his hair; a coarse, wiry mop of a queer grayish-brown. It might well, from its color, be ringed hair; and if it was I should have little doubt of the man's identity. But was it? I was getting on in years and could not see near objects clearly without my spectacles; and I had laid down my spectacles somewhere in the parlor.

"As I lathered his face, I leaned over him to look at his hair more closely, but he shrank away in fierce alarm, and after all my eyesight was not good enough. Once I tried to get out my lens; but he challenged me furiously as to my object, and I put it away again. I dared not provoke him to violence, for if he had struck me I should have killed him on the spot. And he might be the wrong man.

"The operation of shaving him was beset with temptations from moment to moment. Forgotten anatomical details revived in my memory. I found myself tracing through the coarse skin those underlying structures that were so near to hand. Now I was at the angle of the jaw, and as the ringing blade swept over the skin I traced the edge of the strap-like muscle and mentally marked the spot where it crossed the great carotid artery. I could even detect

122

the pulsation of the vessel. How near it was to the surface! A little dip of the razor's beak at that spot—

"But still I had no clear evidence that he was the right man. A mere impression—a feeling of physical repulsion unsupported by any tangible fact—was not enough to act on. One moment a savage impatience for retribution urged me to take the chance; to fell him with a blow and fling him down into the cellar. The next, my reason stepped in and bade me hold my hand and wait for proof. And all the time he watched me like a cat, and kept his hands thrust into the hip pockets of his coat.

"Again and again these mental oscillations occurred. Now I was simply and savagely homicidal, and now I was rational—almost judicial. Now the vital necessity was to prevent his escape; and yet, again, I shrank from the dreadful risk of killing an innocent man.

"What the issue might have been I cannot say. But suddenly the door opened, a burly carter entered and sat down, and the opportunity was gone. The Russian waited for no lengthy inspection in the glass like his predecessor. As soon as he was finished he sprang from the chair, slapped down his coppers in payment and darted out of the shop, only too glad to take himself off in safety. There must have been something very sinister in my appearance.

"The carter seated himself in the chair and I fell to work on him mechanically. But my thoughts were with the man who was gone. What a fiasco it had been! After waiting all these years, I had met a man whom I suspected to be the very wretch I sought; I had actually been alone with him—and I had let him go!

"The futility of it! Before my eyes the grinning tenants of the great wall-case rose in reproach; the little, impassive faces in those shallow boxes seemed to look at me and ask why they had been killed. I had let the man go; and he would certainly never come to my shop again. True, I should know him again; but what better chance should I ever have of identifying him? And then again came the unanswerable question: Was he really the man, after all?

"So my thoughts fluttered to and fro. Constant, only, was a feeling of profound dejection; a sense of unutterable, irretrievable failure. The carter—a regular customer—rose and looked askance at me as he rubbed his face with the towel. He remarked that I 'seemed to be feeling a bit dull tonight,' paid his fee, and, with a civil 'good evening,' took his departure.

"When he had gone I stood by the chair wrapped in a gloomy reverie. Had I failed finally? Was my long quest at an end with my object unachieved? It almost seemed so.

"I raised my eyes and they fell on my reflection in the large mirror; and suddenly it was borne in on me that I was an old man. The passing years of labor and mental unrest had left deep traces. My hair, which was black when I first came to the east, was now snow-white and the face beneath it was worn and wrinkled and aged. The sands of my life were running out apace. Soon the last grains would trickle out of the glass; and then would come the end—the futile end, with the task still unaccomplished. And for this I had dragged out these twenty weary years, ever longing for repose and the eternal reunion! How much better to have spent those years in the peace of the tomb by the dear companion of my sunny hours!

"I stepped up to the glass to look more closely at my face, to mark the crow's-feet and intersecting wrinkles in the shrunken skin. Yes, it was an old, old face; a weary face, too, that spoke of sorrow and anxious thought and strenuous, unsatisfying effort. And presently it would be a dead face, calm and peaceful enough then; and the wretch who had wrought all the havoc would still stalk abroad with his heavy debt unpaid.

"Something on the surface of the mirror interposed between my eye and the reflection, slightly blurring the image. I focussed on it with some difficulty and then saw that it was a group of finger-marks; the prints made by the greasy fingers of my dandy customer when he had leaned on the glass to inspect his teeth. As they grew distinct to my vision, I was aware of a curious sense of familiarity; at first merely subconscious and not strongly attracting my attention. But this state lasted only for a few brief moments. Then the vague feeling burst into full recognition. I snatched out my lens and brought it to bear on those astounding impressions. My heart thumped furiously. A feeling of awe, of triumph, of fierce joy and fiercer rage surged through me, and mingled with profound self-contempt.

"There could be no mistake. I had looked at those finger-prints too often. Every ridge-mark, every loop and whorl of the varying patterns was engraved on my memory. For twenty years I had carried the slightly enlarged photographs in my pocket-book, and hardly a day had passed without my taking them out to con them afresh. I had them in my pocket now to justify rather than aid my memory.

"I held the open book before the glass and compared the photographs with the clearly-printed impressions. There were seven finger-prints on the mirror; four on the right hand and three on the left, and all were identical with the corresponding prints in the photographs. No doubt was possible. But if it had been—

"I darted across to the chair. The floor was still littered with the cuttings from that villain's head. In my idiotic preoccupation with the other man I had let that wretch depart without a glance at his hair. I grabbed up a tuft from the floor and gazed at it. Even to the unaided eye it had an unusual quality when looked at closely; a soft, shimmering appearance like that of some delicate textile. But I gave it only a single glance. Then rushing through to the parlor, I spread a few hairs on a glass slip and placed it on the stage of the microscope.

"A single glance clenched the matter. As I put my eye to the instrument, there, straying across the circular field, were the broad gray stripes, each with its dark line of medulla obscured at intervals by rings of tiny bubbles. The demonstration was conclusive. This was the very man. Humanly speaking, no error or fallacy was possible.

"I stood up and laughed grimly. So much for instinct! For what fools call intuition and wise men recognize for mere slipshod reasoning! I could understand my precious intuition now; could analyze it into its trumpery constituents. It was the old story. Unconsciously I had built up the image of a particular kind of man, and when such a man appeared I had recognized him at a glance. The villainous Tartar face: I had looked for it. The fierce, furtive, hunted manner; the restless suspicion; the mop of grayish-brown

125

hair. I had expected them all, and there they were. My man would have those peculiarities, and here was a man who had them. He, therefore, was the man I sought.

"'O! good old "undistributed middle term!" How many intuitions have been born of you?'

"My triumph was short-lived. A moment's reflection sobered me. True, I had found my murderer; but I had lost him again. That bird of ill omen was still a bird in the bush; in the tangled bush of criminal London. He had said that he would come to me again, and I hoped that he would. But who could say? Other eyes than mine were probably looking for him.

"I suppose I am by nature an optimist; otherwise I should not have continued the pursuit all these years. Hence, having mastered the passing disappointment, I settled myself patiently to wait in the hope of my victim's ultimate reappearance. Not entirely passively, however, for, after the shop was shut, I went abroad nightly to frequent the foreign restaurants and other less reputable places of the East End in the hopes of meeting him and jogging his memory. The active employment kept my mind occupied and made the time of waiting seem less long; but it had no further result. I never met the man; and, as the weeks passed without bringing him to my net, I had the uncomfortable feeling that his hair must have grown and been trimmed by someone else; unless, indeed, he had fallen into the clutches of the law.

"Meanwhile I quietly made my preparations—which involved one or two visits to a ship chandler's—and laid down a scheme of action. It would be a delicate business. The villain was some fifteen years younger than I; a sturdy ruffian and desperate, as I had seen. My own strength and activity had been failing for some time now. Obviously I could not meet him on equal terms. Moreover, I must not allow him to injure me. That was a point of honor. This was to be no trial by wager of battle. It was to be an execution. Any retaliation by him would destroy the formal, punitive character which was the essence of the transaction.

"The weeks sped by. They lengthened into months. And still my visitor made no appearance. My anxiety grew. There were times when I looked at my white hair and doubted; when I almost

126

despaired. But those times passed and my spirits revived. On the whole, I was hopeful and waited patiently; and in the end my hopes were justified and my patience rewarded.

"It was a fair evening early in June—Wednesday evening, I recollect—when at last he came. Fortunately the shop was empty, and again, oddly enough, it was some Jewish holiday.

"I welcomed him effusively. No fierce glare came from my eyes now. I was delighted to see him and he was flattered at the profound impression his former visit had made on me. I began very deliberately, for I could hardly hold the scissors and was afraid that he would notice the tremor; which, in fact, he did.

"'Why does your hand shake so much, Mr. Vosper?' he asked in his excellent English. 'You have not been curling your little finger, hein?'

"I reassured him on this point, but used a little extra care until the tremor should subside; which it did as soon as I got over my first excitement. Meanwhile I let him talk—he was a boastful, egotistical oaf, as might have been expected—and I flattered and admired him until he fairly purred with self-satisfaction. It was very necessary to get him into a good humor.

"My terror from moment to moment was that some other customer should come in, though a holiday evening was usually a blank in a business sense until the Christian shops shut. Still, it was a serious danger which impelled me to open my attack with as little delay as possible. I had several alternative plans and I commenced with the one that I thought most promising. Taking advantage of a little pause in the conversation, I said in a confidential tone:

"'I wonder if you can give me a little advice. I want to find somebody who will buy some valuable property without asking too many questions and who won't talk about the deal afterwards. A safe person, you know. Can you recommend me such a person?'

"He turned in the chair to look at me. All his self-complacent smiles were gone in an instant. The face that looked into mine was the face of as sinister a villain as I have ever clapped eyes on.

"'The person you mean,' he said fiercely, 'is a fence—a receiver. Why do you ask me if I know a fence? Who are you? Are

127

you a spy for the police? Hein? What should I know about receivers? Answer me that!'

"He glared at me with such furious suspicion that I instinctively opened my scissors and looked at the neighborhood of his carotid. But I took his question quite pleasantly.

"'That's what they all say,' I remarked with a foolish smile.

"'Who do?' he demanded.

"'Everybody that I ask. They all say, "What should I know about fences?" It's very inconvenient for me.'

"'Why is it inconvenient to you?' he asked less savagely and with evidently awakening curiosity.

"I gave an embarrassed cough. 'Well, you see,' I said, 'it's this way. Supposing I have some property—valuable property, but of a kind that is of no use to me. Naturally I want to sell it. But I don't want it talked about. I am a poor man. If I am known to be selling things of value, people may make uncharitable remarks and busybodies may ask inconvenient questions. You see my position?' Piragoff looked at me fixedly, eagerly. A new light was in his eye now.

"'What have you got?' he demanded.

"I coughed again. 'Aha!' I said with a smile. 'It is you who are asking questions now.'

"'But you ask me to advise you. How can I if I don't know what you have got to sell? Perhaps I might buy the stuff myself. Hein?'

"'I think not,' said I, 'unless you can write a check for four figures. But perhaps you can?'

"'Yes, perhaps I can, or perhaps I can get the money. Tell me what the stuff is.'

"I clipped away at the top of my speed—and I could cut hair very quickly if I tried. No fear of his slipping away now. I had him fast.

"'It's a complicated affair,' I said hesitatingly, 'and I don't want to say much about it if you're not in the line. I thought you might be able to put me on to a safe man in the regular trade.'

"Piragoff moved impatiently, then glanced at the parlor door.

"'Anyone in that room?' he asked.

"'No,' I answered, 'I live here all alone.'

"'No servant! No one to look after you?' he asked the question with ill-concealed eagerness.

"'No. I look after myself. It's cheaper; and I want so little.'

"The last statement I made in accordance with a curious fact that I have observed, which is that the really infallible method of impressing a stranger with your wealth is to dilate on your poverty. The statement had its usual effect. Piragoff fidgeted slightly, glanced at the shop door and said:

"'Finish my hair quickly and let us go in there and talk about this.'

"I chuckled inwardly at his eagerness. Even his personal appearance had become a secondary consideration. I bustled through the rest of the operation, whisked off the cloth and opened the parlor door. He rose, glanced at his reflection in the glass, looked quickly at the shop door and followed me into the little room, shutting and bolting the door after him.

"I watched him closely. I am no believer in the rubbish called telepathy, but, by observing a person's face and actions, it is not difficult to trace the direction of his thoughts. Piragoff gazed round the room with the frank curiosity of the barbarian, and the look of pleased surprise that he bestowed on the safe and the way in which his glance traveled from that object to my person were easy enough to interpret. Here was an iron safe, presumably containing valuables, and here was an elderly man with the key of that safe in his pocket. The corollary was obvious.

"'Is that another room?' he asked, pointing to the cellar door.

"I threw it open and let him look into the dark cavity. 'That,' I said, 'is the cellar. It has a door opening into the back yard, which has a gate that opens into Bell's Alley. It might be useful. Don't you think so?'

"He did think so; very emphatically, to judge by his expression. Very useful indeed when you have knocked down an old man and rifled his safe, to have a quiet exit at the back.

"'Now tell me about this stuff,' said he. 'Have you got it here?'

"'The fact is,' I said confidentially, 'I haven't got it at all—yet' (his face fell perceptibly at this), 'but,' I added, 'I can get it when I like; when I have arranged about disposing of it.'

"'But you've got a safe to keep it in,' he protested.

"'Yes, but I don't want to have it here. Besides, that safe won't hold it all, if I take over the whole lot.'

"Piragoff's eyes fairly bulged with greed and excitement.

"'What sort of stuff is it? Silver?'

"'There is some silver,' I said, superciliously; 'a good deal, in fact. But that's hardly worth while. You see this stuff is a collection. It belongs, at present, to one of those fools who collect jewelry and church plate; monstrances, jeweled chalices and things of that kind.'

"Piragoff licked his lips. 'Aha!' said he, 'I am that sort of fool myself.' He laughed uneasily, being evidently sorry he had spoken, and continued:

"'And you can get all this when you want it, hein? But where is it now?'

"I smiled slyly. 'It is in a sort of private museum; but where that museum is I am not going to say, or perhaps I may find it empty when I call.'

"Piragoff looked at me earnestly. He had evidently written me down an abject fool—and no wonder—and was considering how to manage me.

"'But this place—this museum—it must be a strong place. How are you going to get in? Will you ring the bell?'

"'I shall let myself in with a latch-key,' I said jauntily.

"'Have you got the latch-key?'

"'Yes, and I have tried it. I had it from a friend who lives there.'

"Piragoff laughed outright. 'And she gave you the latch-key, hein? Ha-ha! but you are a wicked old man. And it is strange too.' He glanced from me to his reflection in the little mirror over the safe; and his expression said as plainly as words, 'Now, if she had given it to me, one could understand it.'

"'But,' he continued, 'when you are inside? The stuff will be locked up. You are skilful, perhaps? You can open a safe, for instance? You have tried?'

"'No, I've never actually tried, but it's easy enough. I've often

130

opened packing cases. And I don't think there is an iron safe. They are wooden cabinets. It will be quite easy.'

"'Bah! Packing cases!' exclaimed Piragoff. He grasped my coat sleeve excitedly. 'I tell you, my friend, it is not easy. It is very difficult. I tell you this. I, who know. I am not in the line myself, but I have a friend who does these things and he has shown me. I have some skill—though I practice only for sport, you understand. It is very difficult. You shall let yourself in, you shall find the stuff locked up, you shall try to open the cabinet and you shall only make a great noise. Then you shall come away empty, like a fool, and the police shall set a watch on the house. The chance is gone and you have nothing.'

"I scratched my head like the fool that he thought me. 'That would be rather awkward,' I admitted.

"'Awkward!' he exclaimed. 'It would be wicked! The chance of a lifetime gone! Now, if you take with you a friend who has skill—hein?'

"'Ah!' I said craftily, 'but this is my little nest egg. If I take a friend I shall have to share.'

"'But there is enough for two. If your safe will not hold it, there is more than you can carry. Besides, your friend shall not be greedy. If he takes a third—or say a quarter? How much is the stuff worth?'

"'The collection is said to be worth a hundred thousand pounds.'

"'A hundred thousand!' gasped Piragoff. He was almost foaming at the mouth. 'A hundred thousand! That would be twenty five for me—for your friend—and seventy-five for you. It is impossible for one man. You could not carry it. My friend,' again he grasped my sleeve persuasively, 'I will come with you. I am very skilful. I am strong. I am brave. You shall be safe with me. I will be your comrade and you shall give a quarter—or even less if you like.'

"He could afford to make easy terms—under the circumstances.

"I reflected awhile and at length said, 'Perhaps you are right. Some of the things are large and gold is heavy—we should leave the silver. It would take two to carry it all. Yes, you shall come with me and bring the necessary tools. When shall we do it? Any night will do for me.'

"He reflected, with an air of slight embarrassment, and then asked:

"'Do you open your shop on Sunday?'

"The question took a load off my mind. I had been speculating on what plan of action he would adopt. Now I knew. And his plan would suit me to a nicety.

"'No,' I said, 'I never open on Sunday.'

"'Then,' said he, 'we will do the job on Saturday night or Sunday morning. That will give us a quiet day to break up the stuff.'

"'Yes. That will be a good arrangement. Will you come here on Saturday night and start with me?'

"'No, no!' he replied. 'That would never do. We must not be seen together. Give me a rendezvous. We will meet near the place.'

"Quite so! It would never do for us to be seen together in Whitechapel where we were both known. The fact might be mentioned at the inquest. It would be most inconvenient for Piragoff.

"'And, look you,' he continued; 'wear a top-hat and good clothes; if you have an evening suit, put it on. And bring a new Gladstone bag with some clothes in it. Where will you meet me?'

"I mentioned Upper Bedford Place and suggested half-past twelve, to which he agreed; and, after sending me out to see that the coast was clear, he took his leave, twisting his waxed mustache as he went out.

"I was, on the whole, very well pleased with the arrangement. Particularly pleased was I with Piragoff's transparent plan for disposing of me. For, now that it really came to action, I found myself shying somewhat at the office of executioner; though I meant to do my duty all the same. But the fact that this man was already arranging coolly to murder me made my task less unpalatable. The British sporting instinct is incurable.

"Piragoff's scheme was perfectly simple. We should go together to the house, we should bring away the spoil—I carrying

132

half—convey it to my premises in Saul Street early on Sunday morning. Then we should break up the 'stuff,' and when our labors were concluded, and I was of no further use, he would knock me on the head. The quiet back gate would enable him to carry away the booty in instalments to his lodgings. Then he would lock the gate and vanish. In a few days the police would break into my house and find my body; and Mr. Piragoff, in his hotel at, say Amsterdam, would read an account of the inquest. It was delightfully simple and effective, but it failed to take into account the player on the opposite side of the board.

"The interval between Wednesday and Saturday was a time of anxious thought and considerable excitement. I went out every night, and had the pleasure of discovering that I was honored by the attendance—at a little distance—of Mr. Piragoff. One evening only I eluded him, and watched him drive off furiously in a hansom in pursuit of another hansom which was supposed to contain me. On that night I visited the museum. Not that I had anything special to do. My very complete and even elaborate arrangements had been made some time before and I now had only to look them over and see that they were in going order; to test, for instance, the brass handle that was connected with the electric main, and see that the well-oiled blocks of a couple of purchase tackles ran smoothly and silently. Everything was in working trim, even to the concussor, stowed out of sight, but within easy reach, in its narrow basket.

"Saturday night arrived in due course. I shut up the shop at nine, put on evening clothes, took the newly-purchased Gladstone and hailed a hansom. I drove, in the first place, to the Criterion Restaurant and dined delicately but substantially, carefully avoiding indigestible dishes. From the restaurant I drove to the museum, where I loitered, making a final inspection of my arrangements, until twenty-five minutes past twelve. Then I came forth and walked quietly to Upper Bedford Place.

"As I turned the corner and looked down the wide thoroughfare the long stretch of pavement contained but a single figure; a dim, dark blot on the gray of the summer night. It moved towards me, and, resolving itself into a definite shape, showed me

133

Piragoff in evening dress, enveloped in a voluminous overcoat and carrying a small hand-bag.

"'You are punctual, Vosper,' he said graciously. 'Shall we make our visit now? Is the house quiet yet? These are not, you see.' He nodded at the boarding-houses that we were passing, several of which still showed lights in the windows.

"'Our house has settled down,' I answered. 'The collector is an early bird. I have just been past it to see that all the lights were out.'

"We walked quickly across the square towards the neighborhood of my house. Piragoff was very affable. He conversed cheerfully as we went and gave a pleasant 'Good night' to a policeman, who touched his helmet civilly in response. When I halted at the door of the museum, he looked about him with a slight frown.

"'I seem to know this place,' he murmured. 'Yes, I have been here before; many years ago. Yes, yes; I remember.'

"He laughed softly as if recalling an amusing incident. I set my teeth, inserted the key and pushed the door open.

"'Enter,' I said. He stepped into the hall. I followed and softly closed the door, slipping up the catch as the lock clicked. It was a small precaution, but enough to hinder a hasty retreat.

"I piloted him through to the museum and switched on a single electric lamp which filled the great room with a ghostly twilight. Piragoff looked about him inquisitively and his eye fell on the long wall-case with the dimly-seen, pallid shapes of the company within it. His face blanched suddenly and he stared with wide-open eyes.

"'God!' he exclaimed, 'what are those things?'

"'Those skeletons?' said I. 'They are part of the collection. The fellow who owns this place hoards all sorts of trash. Come round and have a look at them.'

"'But skeletons!' he whispered. 'Skeletons of men! Ah, I do not like them!'

"Nevertheless he followed me round the room, peering in nervously at the case of skulls as we passed. I walked him slowly past the whole length of the wall-case and he stared in at the twenty-four motionless, white figures, shuddering audibly. I must admit that their appearance was very striking in that feeble light; their poses were so easy and natural and their faces, modeled by broad shadows, so singularly expressive. I was very pleased with the effect.

"'But they are horrible!' gasped Piragoff. 'They seem to be alive. They seem to beckon to one—to say, "Come in here: come in and stay with us." Ah! they are dreadful! Let us go away from them.'

"He stole on tip-toe to the other side of the room and stood positively shaking; shaking at the sight of a mere collection of dry bones. It was amazing. I have often been puzzled by the odd, superstitious fear with which ignorant people view these interesting and beautiful structures. But surely this was an extreme case. Here was a callous wretch who would murder without a scruple a young and lovely woman and laugh at the recollection of the atrocity. And he was actually terrified at the sight of a few irregularly-shaped fragments of phosphate of lime and gelatine. I repeat, it was amazing.

"Piragoff recovered only to develop the ferocity of a frightened ruffian.

"'Where is the stuff, fool?' he demanded. 'Show it to me quickly or I will cut your throat. Quick! Let us get it and go.'

"I watched him warily. These neurotic Slav criminals, when they get into a state of panic, are like frightened cats; very dangerous to be near. And the more frightened, the more dangerous. I must keep an eye on Piragoff.

"'I can open one of the cabinets,' I said.

"'Then open it, pig! Open it quickly! I want to get away from this place!'

"He grinned at me like an angry monkey, and I led him to the secret cupboard. As I very deliberately turned the hidden catches and prepared to take out the panel, I considered whether it was not time to set the apparatus going. For I had prepared a little surprise for Piragoff and I was now rather doubtful how he would take it. Besides, I was not enjoying the proceedings as much as I had expected to. Piragoff's lack of nerve was disconcerting.

"However, I took out the panel and stood by to watch the

result. Piragoff peered into the cupboard and uttered a growl of disappointment.

"'There is nothing there but books and those boxes. Lift the boxes down, pig, and let us see what is in them.'

"I lifted the boxes from the shelf.

"'They are very light,' I said. 'And here are two pistols on top of them.'

"These pistols were the surprise that I had prepared in a spirit of mischief. I had taken them from the pockets of the last two specimens and kept them for the sake of the devices that those two imbeciles had scratched on the butts.

"'Pistols!' exclaimed Piragoff. 'Let me look at them.' He snatched the weapons from the top of the box and took them over to the lamp. Immediately I heard a gasp of astonishment.

"'God! But this is a strange thing! Here is Louis Plotcovitch's pistol! And this other belonged to Boris Slobodinsky! They have been here too!'

"He stared at me open-mouthed, holding the pistols—which I had carefully unloaded—one in each trembling hand. What little nerve he had had was going fast.

"I laid the boxes on a small table and switched on the lamp that hung close over it. High up above the table was one of the cross-beams of the roof. From the beam there hung down two purchase-tackles. The tail-rope of each tackle ended in a noose that was hitched on a hook on the wall, and the falls of the two tackles were hitched lightly over two other hooks. But none of these appliances was visible. The shaded lamp threw its bright light on the table only.

"Piragoff came across the room and laid down the pistols.

"'Open those boxes,' he said gruffly, 'and let us see what is in them.'

"I took off the lid of one; and Piragoff started back with a gasp, but came back, snuffing at the box like a frightened animal.

"'What the devil are these things?' he demanded in a hoarse whisper.

"'They look like dolls' heads,' I answered.

"'They look like dead men's heads,' he whispered,

shudderingly, 'only they are too small. They are dreadful. This collector man is a devil. I should like to kill him.' He glared with horrid fascination at the little dry preparations—there were eight in this box, each in its own little black velvet compartment with its number and date on the label. I opened the second box—also containing eight—and he stared into that with the same shuddering fascination.

"'What do you suppose these dates mean?' he whispered.

"'I suppose,' I replied, 'those are the dates on which he acquired them. Here is another box.' This, the last one, was intended to hold nine heads, but it contained only eight—at present. There was an empty compartment of red velvet in the middle, on either side of which were the heads of the last two specimens, twenty-three and twenty-four.

"I took off the lid and stood back to see what would happen.

"Piragoff stared into the box without speaking for two or three seconds. Suddenly he uttered a shriek. 'It is Boris! Boris and Louis Plotcovitch!'

"His figure stiffened. He stood rigid with his hands on his thighs, leaning over the box, his hair bristling, his white face running with sweat, his jaw dropped; the very personification of horror. And of a sudden he began to tremble violently.

"I looked at him with disgust and an instantaneous revulsion of feeling. What! Should I call in the aid of all those elaborate appliances to dispatch a poor trembling devil like this? I would have none of them. The concussor was good enough for him. Nay, it was too good.

"I reached out behind me and lifted one of the nooses from its hook. Its own weight had nearly closed the loop, for the steel eyelet spliced into the end ran very easily and smoothly on the well-greased rope. I opened the loop wide, and leaning towards Piragoff from behind, quietly dropped it over his shoulders, pulling it tight as it fell to the level of his elbows. He sprang up, but at that instant I kicked away one of his feet and pushed him to the unsupported side, when he fell sprawling face downwards. I gave another tug at the rope, and, as he struggled to get to his feet, I snatched the fall of the tackle from its hook and ran away with it, hauling as I went.

Looking back, I saw Piragoff slowly rise to the pull of the tackle until he was upright with his feet just touching the floor. Then I belayed the fall securely to one of a pair of cleats, and approached him.

"Hitherto, sheer amazement had kept him silent, but as I drew near him he gave a yell of terror. This would not do. Taking the gag from the place where I had hidden it in readiness, I came behind him and slipped it over his mouth where I secured it, cautiously evading his attempts to clutch at me. It was a poor gag—having no tongue-piece—but it answered its purpose, for it reduced his shouts to mere muffled bellowings, inaudible outside.

"Now that the poor wretch was pinioned and gagged and helpless, my feelings urged me to get the business over quickly. But certain formalities had to be observed. It was an execution. I stepped in front of the prisoner and addressed him.

"'Listen to me, Piragoff.' At the sound of his name he stopped bellowing and stared at me, and I continued, 'Twenty years ago a burglar came to this house. He was in the dining-room at two o'clock in the morning preparing to steal the plate. A lady came into the room and disturbed him. He tried to prevent her from ringing the bell. But she rang it; and he shot her dead. I need not tell you, Piragoff, who that burglar was. But I will tell you who I am. I am the husband of that lady. I have been looking for you for twenty years, and now I have caught you; and you have got to pay the penalty of that murder.'

"As I ceased speaking he broke out into fresh bellowings. He wagged his head from side to side and the tears coursed down his ghastly face. It was horrible. Trembling, myself, from head to foot, I took the second noose from its hook, passed it over his head and quickly adjusted it. Then I snatched the second fall and walked away with it, gathering in the slack. As the rope tightened in my hand the bellowings suddenly ceased. I never looked back. I continued to haul until I felt the tackle-blocks come together. I belayed the rope to the second cleat and set a half-hitch on the turns. Then I walked out of the museum and shut the door.

"It had been very different from what I had anticipated. As I sat by the laboratory table with my head buried in my hands, I

138

shook as if I had an ague; my skin was bathed in a cold sweat and I felt that it would have been a relief to weep. I was astonished at myself. Twenty-four of these vermin had I exterminated with a light heart, because the blow was dealt in the heat of conflict; and now, because this wretch had been helpless and unresisting, I was nearly broken with the effort of dispatching him.

"I sat in the dark laboratory slowly recovering and thinking of the long years that had slipped away since the hand of this miscreant had robbed me of my darling. Gradually I grew more calm. But fully an hour passed before I could summon resolution to go back into the museum and satisfy myself that the long-outstanding debt had indeed been paid at last to the uttermost farthing.

"On Monday morning I withdrew from my bank a hundred pounds in notes, which I handed to my landlord's widow—Mr. Nathan had died some years previously—with a note surrendering the shop and house in Saul Street. I emptied the safe and brought away such things as I cared to keep, leaving the rest for Mrs. Nathan. Then I shaved off my ragged beard and white mustache, set my Bloomsbury house in order, pensioned off the sergeant-major (who was now growing an old man) and engaged a set of respectable servants. When the last specimen was finished and put in its place in the museum, my work was done. I had now only to wait quietly for the end. And for that I am now waiting, I hope not impatiently.

"Something tells me that I have not long to wait. Certain new and strange sensations, which I have discussed with my friend Dr. Wharton, seem to herald a change. Wharton makes light of them, but I think and hope he is mistaken. And in that hope I rest content; believing that soon I shall hear the curfew chime steal out of the evening mist to tell me that the day is over and that my little spark may be put out."

THE END